DEATH AND FIRE

A THE EVOLVED SERIES: BOOK 1

A Novel By,
KING ELLIE

Prologue
Xánur

I could never forget when the virus hit the world. Everything ceased, and families were torn apart. At first, it started slowly, a human coughing here and there, but then, they started dropping like flies. They weren't exactly zombies. No, they were worse than that. As old as I was, I had seen dead bodies during wars all over the world, but this wasn't the same thing. No, it drove people apart, and it caused the greatest war to break out forcing people to choose between the humans and the supes.

Us supes came in different forms, sizes, and backgrounds. We weren't all just vampires, Lycans, sirens, or even warlocks. There were us, the original creatures, before the hybrids came along. We, the Nephilim, were of royal blood while the hybrids were the children of the Nephilim. They weren't fully like us, but they possess certain characteristics like us. Over the years, the genes were passed down, but each time it was different. No one really found out what it was, just that the DNA carried a trait of who their descendants were.

When we chose to separate ourselves from the dying humans, all of us originals gathered, separating half of the world and literally splitting the earth horizontally on the equator. We built a fortress from heavenly materials that no human could break through, and we finished it off with an invisible layer of protection that was built by the warlocks. It was a solid plan and fortress for years as we continued to build our society and living life. Many humans had survived and were immune to the virus. They lived amongst us in peace. I ruled over our world for years and years, until I wanted to do something else. Everything was mundane, nothing made me happy, and I wanted to live, so I left sitting on the throne like a pompous king and joined the people. The throne would always be mine as it was my birthright, but right now, I let another royal, Vali, take over. It was time for me to explore our world alongside my best friend, Asar.

****

Years went by, I forgot all about the throne and became one with the people. I lived like them, went to work like them, and laughed like they did, but I was empty inside. Everything changed, the world evolved, and we updated. We were building as the world grew, more supes were born, and some died. The humans that lived amongst us did the same, yet nothing shook the void in me. That's when Asar and I created the Sentinels. We were a team of supes that served to protect the growth of the world. Asar and I traveled around our world, training, teaching, and guiding these men and women to show them how to protect themselves.

Yes, we were a different part of the world, but we needed to always be ready and there needed to be order. Just because we were supes, it didn't mean that we didn't need some direction in our communities, cities, and countries. Asar and I were gone from what was once called the United States but was renamed the North because Canada joined us. We explored like a bunch of kids in a new land, but then, it was time to go back to the North. There was a pull, a force I couldn't get rid of no matter what I did. I drowned myself in all sorts of alcohol and drugs but nothing shook it. That force drove me so mad that even Asar knew we had to go back.

When we landed in L.A., I smiled because that force simmered down leaving me breathing space. Years went by before I felt it again as I trained and taught new sentinels.

Today was the day to welcome those level one sentinels. I smiled as Asar came into the classroom with a line of students behind him. They all had black jumpsuits, combat boots, and a bracelet with a color that matched what they were or who they were a descendant of. Asar's face had the biggest smile I'd ever seen in my life as he announced each student as they stood side by side. Then, a female student ran in the classroom. This one snatched my soul as she ran in the room with her hair a curly mess, her combat boots untied, her bracelet missing, and her jumpsuit hugging her body like a second skin.

Asar cleared his throat, I glanced at him, and then, he spoke to me telepathically.

Your wings are... uh, they are out and flapping.

I slightly turned, noticing that my wings were spread wide calmly flapping as though they should be out. I faced the students again. They were in awe of my wings. Then, my eyes stopped on hers. Her eyes were so beautiful to me; hazel-gray, almond-shaped eyes. A combination of an eye color I had never seen before, and the most beautiful thing happened. Her hair, face, and entire body turned into flames. I was in awe as the flames didn't consume her. Instead, they were part of her. I was speechless. I had nothing else going through my mind except for these words that repeated themselves, until I said it telepathically to Asar.

My mate.

****

Lucinda

I had never in all my life seen a man as gorgeous as this one. I was raised here in L.A., raised amongst different supes in the orphanage. Still, I had never seen anyone like him. His pale blue eyes contrasted with the dirty blonde hair that he wore French braided to his waist. He had a trimmed beard, but it didn't take away from who he was, and then, my heart beat so fast inside my body as he stared at me. I had never been gazed at in this way. I couldn't look away from him, and I don't think I wanted to.

When his wings showed themselves, my fingertips itched to touch and caress them. I couldn't help but sigh at such glory, such royalty in front of me. I knew who he was from the moment I joined the Sentinel program. He was Xánur Helson or what I called him in my head, Xáne. He was the son of the god of death that most people thought was a goddess, but those rumors weren't true. I knew this much from the proper studying I had to do to join this program.

I stood in front of this giant, and I couldn't control my flames as I thought I had over the years. My entire body reacted as I felt them lick on my skin, yet they didn't burn me. Xáne's wings retreated as he took the small steps in my direction. When he stopped in front of me, I craned my neck trying to make sure I saw him through my flames. Usually, they hindered me from seeing anyone up close because they were my defense mechanism, but with him, I could see him clearly. With a scowl on his face, he spoke,

"No need to show off."

His deep voice resonated through each and every bone in my body. There was nothing else that could ever seep through me like his voice. I would always remember it, no matter where I was. I bit my bottom lip, nervous as ever. I shut my eyes trying to call off my flames knowing I had no control over them. When I opened my eyes, I knew they were still there,

"I can't… " I glanced up at him.

"You don't know how to call your flames back?" He asked me with a cocked eyebrow.

I shook my head, embarrassed as ever.

"What's your name?" Xáne eyed me up and down.

"Lucinda Howell, but you can call me Lucy." Not able to look away from his gaze.

Xáne leaned into my face, "I think I'll call you Cin," His eyes turned fully black with stars in them. Then, as fast as they did that, they went back to the normal ones he had before. "Now, learn how to control your flames before you kill someone."

Before I could say a word, the students shuffled out of the room with the other trainer, Asar, as if they knew what was going to happen next. When they were fully out of the room, he stepped in closer pulling me into his arms. He transformed in front of me as the man that stood before me disappeared and another creature appeared. His wings enveloped me as my flames threatened to grow. I couldn't stop looking into those eyes. They were even more enticing now, "You are the most beautiful creature I have ever seen," I said breathlessly while my flames licked my skin.

As Xáne smiled, his fangs came out to play while he watched me.

"I'm a natural born devil, let you be the light that converts me," he effortlessly said to me despite the fangs.

My poor heart couldn't take this. He didn't know me, and I didn't know him, but we both knew the force that pulled us together.

KING ELLIE

It felt so natural being here with him and like this. Death and Fire.

Chapter 1
Xánur

My heart was racing once again, and I knew why. I had the same damn dream for the third time this week. I didn't need to dream about her again. I didn't want to see her anymore. It's been three years, but she won't leave my subconscious. What the hell am I supposed to do about that? How do I get rid of her?

Those hazel-gray eyes spoke volumes to me in my dreams. They always looked at me as though they missed me, but I knew better. I resented them the most because I loved them the most about her. Those almond-shaped eyes would always look my way, and I couldn't turn away. They would trap me, and I would lose all sights of anything else. What were the last words she said to me?

Oh yeah, I love you.

Such traitorous words made me want to vomit. Can't she just disappear and not visit me at a time where I wished to be rid of her?

This house, my house. One of the royal homes of the Nephilim left roaming the earth. My father is a fallen angel who loved to populate the world with his seed. Unfortunately, I was the last born who was still alive from his line. There were many supernatural creatures here on the other side of the world...

I lost focus of that as she came into view again laying down beneath me on my bed with rose petals showering all over her body. She was my favorite to stare at. I could stare at her brown skin that resembled a Hershey's kiss, her eyes, her lips that I always wanted to kiss on, and then, the rest of her body. A body that set me on fire each time, yet nothing could get me off her. I loved to show her how much I wanted her, from the moment she let me the first time until the last time.

She was everything to me, that's why I hated her so passionately. The look in her eyes was mesmerizing as she called out to me each time I made love to her.

"Xáne…Xáne," she called my name like a prayer, and there I stood like a dummy eating it all up, but that night, she left me.

She never looked back or said goodbye to me. That's when the dreams started. I would see her beneath me, but right after, she was consumed by the very flames she could conjure out of her body. She was a hybrid, a special one. Her mother was a fire-breathing dragon Nephilim, and her father was a human.

"Cin…" My nickname for Lucinda. I called her out in my dreams, but she couldn't hear me.

My fire, my flame, yet she let them consume me and burn me to a crisp. I would hate her for the rest of my life if I could. That was something I, Xánur Helson, last born son of who the Norse called Hel, the god of death, would never forget. If I could bring her death, I would.

****

I was jolted out of my sleep when I felt a piercing in my side. I didn't scream in pain or anything. It wasn't the first time my girlfriend, Jaya stabbed me in her sleep. She had this thing about sleeping with her knives, and sometimes it was cute or funny to see her try to hurl them at me during training, but right now, it was not funny. I told her a million times that if she weren't human, I would've killed her had I not had any damn self-control. I was a damn vampire, so it didn't take me long to heal but fuck it hurt like hell.

I sat up quickly before she attacked again. She had the same routines as she did when she was fighting. I jumped out of bed not wanting to have to restrain her. I moved over to the edge of the bed watching her in my California sized king bed. How she always gravitated towards me made no damn sense. She had all this space, yet she hogged the entire bed. She was a descendant of the Amazonians, but along the way, she must've lost the power that came with the bloodline. Jaya was one of the million humans left alive after the disease took them years ago. The disease changed their entire earth but us, the supernatural, were able to escape it as it took more than a common airborne virus to kill us off.

Jaya smiled in her sleep as though she knew she succeeded getting me off the bed. She was beautiful with her big, brown eyes, her soft, tanned skin, brunette hair that she kept short in a pixie cut, and she was almost six feet tall. She was built like an Amazonian woman as well, unlike... No! I stopped my mind from wandering to the one person that could ruin my day even without her presence there.

Just then, there was a surge as it traveled from my toes all the way to the roots of my dirty blonde hair. The last time I felt this way was when I had Lucinda beneath me, and she was so overwhelmed with emotions that she couldn't control herself. She set me on fire consuming every part of me, but I didn't stop, I couldn't stop. I shouldn't have stopped because that night she wouldn't have left. I never regretted that moment because I tatted my body up from collarbone to ankles with masterpieces mapping out my life. There was one tattoo of her, and that was placed over my heart sin in big letters because at the time, I was heartbroken, and I thought she was coming back to me.

The alarms began blaring all over town, and my black wings came out because of the shock. I could feel it in the air, and something was up. I shut my eyes letting all the sound in and focusing on the furthest place which was the gate to enter the town. I heard multiple heartbeats, and then, the one thing I never thought I would hear again.

"Guess who just tried to come back in? Lucinda Howell. Take her to quarantine and make sure you alert the captain," one soldier said.

"Fuck!" I screamed out shocking myself.

Jaya jolted up.

"What? What is it!" The alarms blaring didn't wake up, but my shouting did.

I shook my head. I ran my fingers through my shoulder-length hair gazing up at my ceiling.

"I have to go take care of someone that just snuck in," I shut my eyes, my body already reacting to her as the closer she got the tether between us, that we could never break, it began erratically humming. "I am the captain, after all."

I sighed, walking away not able to look Jaya in the eye. Somehow, I knew something was going to happen with Cin back on this side of the gate, but one thing that wouldn't happen was me ever forgiving her.

****

Lucinda

I can't believe I got caught coming back when I never got caught leaving. I inhaled deeply. I missed the air on this side. It was different; contained as we were covered by an invisible fortress that couldn't be seen since it was so high up. The gate wasn't some crazy looking thing, it was red-brick built and high enough to reach the skies with a magical door that only the sentinels knew how to open, but I had a crawl space. I should've known that I was going to get caught. I looked up at the sky as the blue stood out and the clear clouds unlike the other side of the wall that was full of smoke, carcasses everywhere, some humans staggered to stay alive because the virus hadn't fully killed them as we thought.

I took a deep breath knowing I had no right to come back but where else was I going to go? I selfishly left everything behind because I had to find my parents. I wanted to believe my father was out there with my mother before they sent me off here to be part of this side of the world, but I fooled myself. My parents were nowhere to be found. All that was left were just dead, rotting bodies, waste polluted the open side of the earth that contained only humans who couldn't beat this. I contemplated for three years if I should come back and after realizing how alone I truly was, I came back with my tail tucked between my legs, figuratively speaking of course.

"Why do you have to call me out here when you can handle this yourselves… huh? What are you guys getting paid for, if it isn't this?" He yelled.

I heard his voice before I righted my head in his direction. I could never forget my mate's voice. My entire body froze, I knew what I was avoiding deep within me. The vibrant humming of our tether as I got closer and closer to this side of the world, I felt him, but I couldn't read his emotions until now as his pale-blue eyes met mine. He hated me. The emotion hummed so loudly that I could've sworn those around us felt it.

"Why is she here? Who allowed her in?" Xáne's voice caused my heart to skip a beat, but the icy stare in his eyes let me know that he didn't want to see me.

If he could kill me, he would, and I would let him. That sounded crazy, but that's how much I loved this man. He didn't get it, he would've never let me go out there alone, and I needed to do this journey on my own. He is my everything, but the way he watched me told me so much more than I wanted to admit. I hurt him; I really did. It was killing me that he had changed physically as well. He was even much more handsome than he was three years ago. He grew out of his younger looking body, and now, he stood tall like a man.

His kind grew up differently, looking young for a long time and aging slowly. His hair wasn't down his back anymore. It was shoulder-length now. His bushy, naturally arched eyebrows told you how he felt before he even said it. I used to joke with him telling him that his eyebrows always told me how he felt about a situation. He no longer had a beard, and his jawline was impeccable. It showed off his best features and his lips; the bottom fuller than the top. The bottom lip was like a cushion for his fangs. His entire body was beautiful in a gray t-shirt that hugged his upper body like a second skin, and those dark jeans didn't help it either. Xáne was definitely not the younger looking man I left three years ago. A man was standing in front of me now. He was bigger in size which made him look taller than his freakishly six- foot-eight inches.

I sighed hoping to God that he wouldn't kick me back out there. Xáne eyed me from the top of my head to the dirty shoes on my feet, and he scowled. I don't remember the last time I bathed, cut my hair, or even ate. I could feel his disgust, and it made me want to cower away from him. He once thought of me as beautiful, and right now, I knew he didn't believe that. Before anything else could transpire, a female stepped even closer to him, and I blinked. Did I not notice her this whole time? She was hard to miss. She was huge, much taller than my five-foot-two self. She looked ready to eat me alive from her toned arms to her toned legs as she pulled off her sentinel outfit well.

When my eyes followed her hand that was in Xáne's, I forgot that I was the reason for this and flipped the fuck out. I heard as the sentinels who were holding me tight shrieked. I knew my body came alive with the flames that licked my skin. I couldn't see or think straight, all I knew was that my mate was being touched by someone else. I was selfish, I know, but to see someone else touching him and him allowing it, I couldn't breathe correctly.

Everything in me was losing all the fake calm resolve I had when I got caught. It was all unleashing, and I felt like a wounded bird that got kicked some more instead of being helped.

"Enough!" I heard Xáne, but he didn't get it.

His tether was making me break out into hives. I felt how he wanted to protect her from me. He wasn't in love with her, but he deeply liked her. I went down to my knees. I couldn't breathe as I felt my flames expand. This couldn't be happening. He was mine!

"Mine!" I screeched out like a wounded animal. This entire side and the abandoned side of the world could hear my claim on this man, and I didn't care.

I am not yours anymore. He spoke to me telepathically through our bond.

That increased my flames causing my insides to feel the lick of the flames, then there was this twisting in my gut as I felt Xáne close himself off to me. No, he didn't break the tether, but the humming suddenly stopped and what I felt as comfort all along, was him, and now, I was empty.

Everything stopped, as I dropped to the ground everything became blurry. I couldn't see anything right, but what was clear was that I was going to kill the girl, whether she was the sweetest girl ever or not because no matter what, Xáne belonged to me.

****

When I woke up, I was trapped, naked in a glass box barely able to stand. I couldn't place anything. Had things changed that much since I'd been gone? Didn't they keep the supes that couldn't be controlled in boxes like these? There were so many questions going through my mind, yet none of them could be answered because I was alone. I checked out the room they kept me in, no this wasn't a room, it was a prison within a prison. There were no doors. The walls were painted all white with the padding making it look like this was a room for those who were insane. I wanted to stand but sitting was for the best, they knew what they were doing.

"Let me out of here!!" I yelled… and yelled for hours on end, yet no one came in.

I didn't want to be in here. This wasn't fair. What was going on and why were they doing this to me? As if someone heard me, there was an opening that I hadn't spotted before.

"Shut up!"

"Xáne," I said his name as though it was a prayer on my lips and the only way to get into heaven was to say it over and over again.

I was afraid to gaze up into his face as he came closer, the lights turned off, and the room became pitch black. I shuddered, he knew how much I didn't like the dark. I was afraid of it much more than anything else in the world.

His voice traveled to my left ear,

"You don't have a right to say my name like that? Did you think you could just sneak back in and all would be alright?" Each word was laced with venom.

I wouldn't cry or break my resolve again. I shut my eyes as I called on my fire. I had to see where I was. I didn't like this. When I called to my fire, the temperature dropped significantly. I had never felt this kind of cold before, but now, it ran through my veins dwindling my fire. I opened my eyes staring down at my fingertips as the sparks died out there, too. How could he take this from me?

"I'm sorry," this is what I needed to tell him.

"I don't want your sorry bit-," Xáne stopped. He didn't say it.

He was right to want to call me that, I was a bitch but to know that he couldn't utter those words through his lips made me smile. That expression didn't stay on my face too long as he appeared in front of me in the blink of an eye, and I made the mistake of turning his way. I knew better than to gaze into those eyes, yet the willpower that I thought I had was being the bitch right now as it cowered away in the corner of the room. I didn't even notice that the glass box was gone, what was that?

"Xánur…" I called his name out, and the next thing I knew, his hand wrapped around my throat.

"What did I just say?" He asked me as he got all up in my face. "Don't utter my name. It isn't yours to say."

The flames seemed to ignite again. This was always the problem, Xáne knew how to call them out without my permission. It was the skin to skin contact. I was pissed. I apologized, what more could I do? I reached out to his chest and tried to push him off me.

"What am I supposed to address you as… huh! I said I was fucking sorry! What the fuck!" At that moment, I forgot that I was the one who wronged him. I got all up in his face, "You want to kill me Xánur?" I gritted my teeth.

His big, black wings expanded filling up half of the room. No matter what, I was always fascinated by them. I didn't need the tether to know that his next words were the truth.

"You always thought you could one-up me, don't you?" I noticed he hadn't called out my name. I wanted to hear him say it, but I knew he wouldn't give me that. Xáne gave me a million-dollar smile, the one he gave those that he would rip their heads from the bodies. I felt the chill that passed in the room. "You'll wish you were dead instead of coming back here."

He let me go standing as though he hadn't just threatened me. He turned away to leave, and my mouth spoke faster than my brain could process, "If you think I'm going to go down easily, then you've got another thing coming. You're mine, Xáne."

He threw his head back laughing as though I was a goddamn comedian, "You're going to wish I was never yours, mate." He said it as though it was an insult even to be his mate.

The hatred hummed through the tether knocking me to my back. I guess the tether controlled us, instead of the other way around. The glass box appeared again before I could even sit up.

"Fuck!" I banged on the glass door not letting up even as my fists began bleeding from the impact, "Let me out of here!"

Chapter 2
Xánur

Didn't I deserve a fucking break from this bullshit? My body was on fire as if she had touched me from the moment, I wrapped my hand around her throat. I always knew I could conjure up her flames, she was my human flame, but I wanted her to feel what it felt like to have something that was a part of you dwindle down and die. Usually, if any of my friends came up to me and said this, I would call them pussies but fuck that. Cin didn't deserve anything but this hatred from me. I didn't give two shits what her excuses were for this mess. All I knew was that she was not going to stomp her little ass around telling me I was hers when that was over and done with.

I knew deep down that I would never stop loving this girl, but she wasn't mine anymore. I wanted nothing to do with her, and she needed to know that much.

"Xánur!" I heard my name being called out. I turned from staring into nothingness instead of the perfect view of the night sky in my office.

There, Jaya was still in her black on black sentinel outfit. Why was she still here?

"You're not done working yet?"

She cleared her throat as I noticed she was with the trainee.

"Well, Captain Helson, I was showing Marla how things went around here. Shouldn't you be gone for the day?" Jaya watched me.

I knew what she was trying to say. It had been two weeks since I last went down there to see Cin, and I knew she was going crazy because our tether didn't shut off as I wanted it to. It was driving me insane, all her emotions were driving me up the wall. Her flames felt like they were licking my skin and touching me in every way trying to caress it. This had never happened before when we were together, but this time around, seeing each other again must've sparked something else because ever since I touched her, I couldn't get her flames off my skin.

"I'll be going in a bit, I jus-," I threw my head back as my wings spread so violently as if they were being ripped from my body.

My fangs protruded, and I was so sure that my pale blue eyes were no longer there and that my eyeballs were all black.

"Xánur! What is it?" I could hear Jaya moving closer, but she couldn't come near me like this. If she touched me, I would kill her. This always happened.

"Don't!" I stumbled back as my wings tried to fly away.

My wings were flapping, knocking everything off my desk. Papers were flying around, and I knew where they were trying to go. I didn't stop to hear anyone as I ran out of my office at full force. Neither Marla or Jaya could keep up, but they would catch up when they figured out where I was headed. Something was wrong with Cin, and my instincts screamed louder than anything else. I tried to resist, but my wings pushed me to keep going or else everything in this damn building would come down.

I heard Cin's screams, and I lost it. I roared like a wounded beast as I got to the door of where she was kept in, in less than a minute. I've never used my teleportation here before this moment and I had taken a moment to realize why things could go differently, but this wasn't the time. I ripped the door open searching around for her. Someone had turned the lights on, dropped the temperature lower than I had it when I saw two of my biggest sentinels holding her down as another reared his fist back and struck her. The side of my face stung, and I gritted my teeth. The moment I levitated shouldn't have ever been witnessed by so many people, but they pushed me.

The reason I was a Helson, death's son, came to pass in this very room. The sentinels weren't weak men either. They were strong, trained Lycans, but compared to me, a vamp who has lived for years yet looked so young, they thought I was inexperienced even as their boss. I inhaled, shutting my eyes as I triggered them to shift. They didn't know I could do this, well now was a good of a time as any other.

All three Lycans screamed as they shifted. I made sure that they felt each bone breaking and reshaping as though it was their first time shifting. They sounded like wounded animals, and I didn't give two shits. I heard Jaya and Marla as they made it to the door, but they both stopped in their steps. I shifted my gaze towards Jaya, the shock was there as I saw my reflection in her eyes. I had completely shed my human skin, and I resembled Hel. I was the color of my black wings; black from head to toe, there was nothing that looked human on me. Not the large talons that replaced my hands and feet, nor the velvety skin that took over. My fangs were proud to make an appearance at this moment. I faced the Lycans as their transformation was complete, and I landed on the ground with a thud that shook the building.

I lifted a talon beckoning the first one to come and charge me. The fear was in his eyes, so before he could even think about running out, I charged him. Everyone would know never to touch Cin. She was mine to torture and to kill when I was good and ready to do so. Time slowed for me as I broke each Lycan's bones one by one. I didn't stop until each body part was pulled from them and their blood coated every part of this white room. This is what they wanted to do to Cin, and these were the consequences. I laughed wholeheartedly as the last Lycan tried to stand tall with half of his limbs missing.

"Tonight, you served your purpose. Let this be an example for those who think they could touch what doesn't belong to them," I know what my voice sounded like at this moment.

It was sinister, and it was down-right terrifying. I've made grown supes cry with the simple threat that came with this voice when I was like this. This was a warning to each and every one on this side of the world. If I had to lay waste to it so that no one touched her, then so be it.

As everything stopped, I made my way towards Cin. She laid there on the ground, naked as ever. I watched her, something was different about her, off even. Her body was painted with scars that seemed to have healed over time, she was much shapelier than I remembered. My eyes spotted a long scar on her lower abdomen. Who did that to her? Before I could stop myself, I was on my knees, my fingers itching to touch the scar. I shouldn't have done that, but the moment I traced the scar, memories flooded my mind, exploding with images of Cin pregnant as she walked around. Sick humans grabbed her ankles trying to get her to help them up, others yelled at her as green spit flew everywhere out of their mouths, and she ran. Then, the next scene, someone who remained faceless cut her open delivering a baby, yet when Cin held it, I knew there was no life there. She mourned that baby, our baby, and I snatched my fingers away from her scar.

I stumbled back, not stopping until I was on the other end of the room away from a passed out Cin. Everything in me went rigid. What the fuck happened to her in the last three years?

****

Lucinda

When I woke up, it took me a while to remember what happened. I opened my eyes looking around. I wasn't in that white room anymore or in that glass cell. My eyes took the room in. It looked like a regular hospital room, but I knew better. There was no way Xáne was going to let me go anywhere he couldn't find and threaten me. What was going on with me? My memories were all jumbled up. When I left, I didn't think that Xáne would be this mad at me. I figured he'd cool down and eventually understand that I had to, but at this moment, I knew how much of a grudge he could keep. If he wanted to hate you, he could forever hate you, and there was nothing you could do to rectify that situation. So, then why did I leave like that?

As I thought of why I would ever do such a thing, a buzzing sound rang deep and high in my head. I gritted my teeth through the pain. Something wasn't right, and I could feel it. I would never leave Xáne like that, I didn't even leave a note or something. I couldn't remember the couple of days before I left, nothing was coming to me. All I remembered was leaving Xáne as he slept with a strong determination that he couldn't know and that he would forgive me.

The pain in my head passed, giving me a chance to breathe properly again. I shut my eyes. The brightness of the lights and the room brought the headache back. I heard footsteps but didn't make a sound as they got closer to my bedside.

"Mrs. Helson? Mrs. Helson?" At first, I didn't think he was talking to me, but then I remembered that Xáne and I were mated and married.

No one had called me by that last name in a long time that I didn't even notice when the sentinels called me by my former last name, Howell, but now, the reality of this situation came crashing hard on me. I didn't just leave some man, I left the love of my life, my mate, my husband behind. No wonder why he wants to kill me. We were supes, and I knew better, yet I didn't have a clue as to why I didn't do better.

The man's palm touched my bare arm. It was warm to the touch, but I refused to move, "Mrs. Helson, I know you're awake. I'm a vamp. I can hear your heart beating a mile a minute. Now, can you open your eyes and look at me?" He pleaded with me, and slowly, I opened my eyes.

When I opened my eyes, I almost cried tears of joy. I gasped as my best friend, Xáne's cousin, Asar Ragna was in front of me. He smiled. He was still beautiful. His midnight blue hair still French-braided down to his waist. Eyes, the color of the night sky when it is full of stars, the sharpest jawline, one that rivaled Xáne's, the body of a soldier, and almost the same height as his cousin. All the royals were taller than ever.

"Asar…" I was so sorry to him, too. I didn't even say goodbye to my best friend. He had been there for me through everything.

"My poor little flame," His fingers reached out caressing my cheek. "You've been missed," his accent was like Xáne's, unable to be placed.

I sighed knowing that there was someone who wanted to speak to me.

"I'm so sorry," tears ran down my cheeks without my consent.

Asar didn't even think twice about it as he pulled me up for a hug. My body wasn't in as much pain as I thought it would be. Someone healed me, and it was probably Asar, the only person who truly wanted me alive.

"Oh, you little cry baby, it's alright. You've missed so much, but nothing between us changes. You are my best friend and I, yours. You're coming home with me," he stated.

I pulled out of the hug, stunned that Xáne would ever let me go after he promised to kill me.

"He's letting me go?"

Asar eyed me up and down,

"Will he ever let you go Cin? Just know I struck up a deal to keep you with me and you can never leave this side of the earth again."

I narrowed my eyes, there was no way he was letting me go so easily, and as if he heard me summon him, Xáne's footsteps alerted me that he was in the room. My eyes followed wherever he was, as they always did.

"You're letting me go Xáne?" He flinched at his name being said on my lips.

A couple of other footsteps joined his side, and I looked up to see a few sentinels and that girl. I gritted my teeth trying to stay neutral for fear he'd lock me up in that box again and keep me in the dark.

"Asar," Xáne said his name with venom dripping from his lips. "He will be in charge of you. You will continue where you left off before you walked out of here leaving everything behind like an irresponsible child."

At the mention of the word, child, I flinched, and Xáne noticed. Sorrow enveloped me, his emotions not mine, were flooding me and they were overwhelming. He glanced down, I followed where he was looking. I was happy that I wasn't naked, but with the way he was gazing at me, I might as well be. I hope to God, he didn't know what happened while I was away. I forced myself not to conjure up the memory, I didn't want Xáne to know. I felt like this was my burden to bear alone.

"What Captain Helson is saying, is that you are on lockdown," the warrior bitch spoke up as if she was his mouthpiece. I rolled my eyes not even holding back. "You are to be with Asar at all times when you are not continuing your education. Seeing that you didn't finish your sentinel program as per your kind, you will join level one again. You will be the oldest there as the others are in their early twenties and you are what? Thirty?"

The fuck? Was she serious right now? I'm twenty-seven thank you very little. I gritted my teeth as I controlled my flames. If she were a dude, I'd punch her in the nuts. Hard. She probably still had nuts from the looks of it. Xáne and Asar coughed like a bunch of immature boys trying not to laugh. I forgot they were the only ones that were linked to me telepathically. Xáne as my mate and Asar as my protector.

Asar's hand lightly gripped my jaw, and he made me face him. He lightly shook his head although the amusement was written all over his face.

"She'll do that, and I'll make sure of it," Asar answered before I could tell all of them to kiss my ass.

"Good," Xáne answered and walked out without so much as a second glance my way, but my eyes always followed him. I don't think they could ever stop doing so. Ever.

Chapter 3
Xánur

The moment I watched Asar come in the room with a smile on his face, I knew I was having a Déja Vu moment. Level one trainees came in, this time in the training area that was too big for its own good. Each one walked behind the other, and when they stood side by side waiting for my instructions, my eyes found hers. Even now, with her black hair straight reaching her shoulders, her chocolate skin was glistening, and her body still filling that black jumpsuit well. I cleared my throat not wanting to concentrate on Cin, but it was hard especially with the way she looked at me. She gazed at me as if this was the first time she had laid eyes on me. She didn't smile nor frown; Her emotions poured not only through the tether but the way she tilted her head staring at me. It was unnerving. I blinked shaking my head trying to concentrate on everyone else.

I loudly clasped my hands together getting her attention, and she seemed to notice what she was doing. Cin looked away bashfully, I felt the tugging of my lips as a small smile appeared on my face.

Is that a smile on your face dear cousin? It's been so long.

Asar spoke to me telepathically, I glared at him, scowling in the process.

No.

I answered him then shut him out for the time being.

I watched each and every student that came in, there was about fifteen of them this time around. The schooling was over with, and now it was training time. There were only two levels, but each level had a different series of tests that they needed to pass with both skills and powers.

"Alright, everyone. First off, welcome to Level one training. Now, if I could have you standing in with your kind," I watched them as they each followed the rules.

We had three vampires, three Lycans, five sirens, three humans, and then the oddball out, Cin. I sighed, she was the only one left of her kind, and that's why Asar was her protector.

"I, uh," she spoke up. "I'm kinda short on a group here. Kinda awkward." She did that nervous chuckle and tucked her hair behind her left ear.

Asar as her protector decided to switch it up,

"let's do this, there's us, three instructors," I looked to where he was pointing to his left, and there Jaya stood. I hadn't noticed she came in. "So, everyone pair up and as for you Cin, you go with the only person who can put out your flames, Xánur.

Asar smirked as he winked my way. He walked off to the other trainees pairing them off as Cin made her way towards her. I watched as she purposefully walked in front of Jaya, swinging her hips in a dramatic fashion. I narrowed my eyes at her knowing what the hell she was doing. Jaya gritted her teeth as she tried to focus on anything else but Cin and as she stopped in front of me, Jaya screamed as a small flame appeared on her shoulder. She patted her shoulder putting it out in less than a second.

I leaned down getting all up in Cin's face,

"Cut that shit out!" I harshly whispered.

She scoffed.

"I didn't mean to do it," she was playing coy with me.

I narrowed my eyes not paying attention to those around us as I got even more into her space.

"You're so full of shit, and I know you well enough to know you enjoyed doing that."

Cin opened her mouth to respond, but we were interrupted by Asar giving the okay for us to begin our training. I grinned at her as my arms flew out gripping both her wrists twisting them behind her. She shrieked, and I ate it up. I kept her there for a moment as she struggled.

"You're cheating!" She accused me.

I cocked an eyebrow letting her go abruptly causing her to fall on the floor that was covered with mats. I backed up a bit giving her space. I lifted my hand calling her over to me with my finger, "if you think I'm cheating, come over here and beat me. My size shouldn't scare you."

Cin glared at me as she stood on her feet. She got in a fighting stance just like I taught her so long ago. My chest swelled with pride, my teachings helped her survive out there. She took this opportunity to charge first, and that was her biggest mistake, thinking that I didn't know her well. But then again, if I knew her so well, wouldn't I have known she was planning on leaving me?

Fuck! I needed to let it go because I had moved on, hadn't I?

****

As we got into the rhythm of fighting, all else was lost to us. This was always Cin and my problem, when we were immersed in each other, we'd often forget about those around us. It wasn't fair to them, but this was us except there wasn't an us this time around. I didn't even think as I grabbed her wrists again this time dropping with her to the mats.

"This is so cheating!" Cin said as she tried to wiggle her legs from under the lock, I put her entire body in.

"Is it?" I questioned.

"Uh yeah. It's cause you're bigger and you just had to go take your shirt off. You know that's my weakness! The damn nerve of you to get your whole upper body tatted," she rambled when she was nervous. "speaking of tattoos, that's sin one," She gestured with her head.

I growled as I got all up in her face,

"what about it? You got a problem with it?"

Cin's eyes went cartoon character wide, it was comical, yet the heat that was coming from her body threw me off. No, her flames didn't appear. This was her body heat wanting me to touch and caress her like I used to. I was enamored by her eyes as the flames appeared in them instead of her body, it was fascinating to witness.

"When did that start?" I whispered.

"What?" She breathlessly asked.

"The flames in your eyes?"

"Oh! After I lost our ..." she stopped talking then. The flame disappeared from her eyes and tears fell from her eyes faster than anything else.

I was caught off guard by them. I hadn't seen her cry in so long that it tugged at my heart.

"Please," her voice cracked. "let me go. I have to go."

I ignored that. I wanted her to tell me what we had lost, I had to hear it from her mouth.

"After we lost our what Lucinda?"

Her breath hitched. She knew when I called her name like that, it was usually in an intimate setting. Just her and I but I didn't care right now. She was crying, and I itched to comfort her. The tether was a bitch at times, like now when it almost broke my resolve with the amount of sorrow and heartbreak that consumed me.

Cin broke down now in serious tears,

"please Xáne, let me go."

My anger came back full blown as I let her go standing with her. I masked all the other emotions that threatened to show themselves as I stared into her teary eyes,

"I let you go already. You don't ever have to beg me to do it twice."

I walked off after that as I heard her sobs getting louder haunting my every step out of that damn room and into the hallway.

Why did it seem like I hurt her when I wasn't the one who left?

I heard footsteps behind me, they were heavy, and it was Asar.

"I let her go back to my office. I'll take her home. Don't worry cousin, I'll take care of her," he assured me.

I stared, concentrating on the empty hallway full of beige walls.

"I don't give a shit what you do with her," I spoke through gritted teeth.

"Yes, you do." His words rang true, and I hated him for it.

I spun to my left punching the wall knowing that it would leave a gigantic hole in it.

"I would've done any and everything for her, so why did she fucking leave me?" I shouted facing my cousin with my right knuckle bleeding, it would heal in a moment. "Can you answer that Asar? Huh?"

I know I must've appeared crazed, yet Asar remained calm. He didn't say anything, or rather, he didn't have an answer for that either.

I scoffed,

"I fucking thought so. Fuck her for breaking my heart, and yes, I'm man enough to say it. She took my fucking heart, and I will never forgive her for that... not ever!" I stormed off not giving a shit who heard me in the process.

****

Lucinda

She took my fucking heart, and I will never forgive her for that... I tossed and turned as I tried to sleep for the seventh night after training. Xáne refused to look at me in the eye as he trained me. He didn't speak to me unless he was giving me instructions, and it hurt me much more than I wanted to admit. I sighed, rolling over to face the window in my room. He didn't know how much I dreamt of him when I was out there all alone. He was the only reason why I kept going and didn't give in. I could've just died, but I didn't want to because I owed it to Xáne to come back. I should've known and should've realized that his anger would be different and much more untamed, but I was foolish.

I shut my eyes thinking of the way he laughed when he thought something was funny. He was carefree around me, but now, he couldn't stand the sight of me. I was repulsive to him. I wanted to accept that and move on, but who would I move on with? I shuddered calming my flames as the thought of him being with Jaya in the same bed came to mind.

I hope he gets whiskey dick, so he can't fuck her.

I said to no one in particular, and I heard Asar laughing in the next room over.

Oh, my darling Cin, I can guarantee you that the moment you sneaked back in, he can't get it up for anyone else but you.

I lightly chuckle.

I freaking wish, but he hates me too much even to want to touch me during training.

It was weird, through our telepathic communication, I could feel a smile when it appeared on Asar's face.

That's called self-restraint and punishment. If you desire to be touched, my dear Cin, I can come cuddle with you.

Before I could respond to Asar, Xáne broke through our communication.

You fucking touch her, and you're dead. Now, can you both shut up and Cin, stop tossing and turning. Go to sleep! Fuck!

I giggled not able to help myself. I felt warmth envelop me like a blanket as I shut my eyes. Suddenly, I was feeling really sleepy.

And just so you both know, I never get whiskey dick. Don't disrespect me like that.

I felt as Xáne flipped over in his bed in the same direction that I was in, as though he was there pulling me into his arms so that I could fall asleep and that was precisely what I did.

****

I knew I was dreaming when someone screamed. I turned my head towards the noise, and automatically, I was back there again, on the other side of the world, the damaged and dying part. I tried to breathe through the noise and the pain of seeing how the humans died off. I walked along a metal fence and there was a human that was split in two. She looked up at me. Her eyes were dead, yet it was as if she was still breathing. I gasped putting my hand over my mouth not wanting anyone to hear me out here. I clutched my growing belly. Why had I left home to search for a family that was nowhere to be found?

I searched for my parents everywhere, but it was a dead end. Now, here I was, pregnant as ever with no one to help in this difficult situation I put myself in. My heart ached, and I missed Xáne. I thought missing him would get easier, but it was months after, and I couldn't shake it off. I loved this man with every fiber of my being. Why did I leave without telling him again? As I tried to think of the reason why a ringing sound erupted in my head. I clutched my head in both my hands screaming. The pain physically hurt as though someone took a bat or something swinging it making sure to crack my skull.

My screeching caught the attention of the dying humans, but I didn't care about them coming closer to me. I couldn't do this anymore. This was too much. I wanted to give up, yet at the same time, I couldn't do this to my child. I took a deep breath calling out my flames. They refused to obey me ever since I left my mate. I concentrated on my memories of Xáne, even if he couldn't feel me reaching out to him, I wanted him to be the last person I saw before I died. As I thought of him, our last night together, our love, and what our love produced. Then, my flames erupted from my skin. This was the hottest I had ever had them. I opened my eyes remembering what he taught me. I noticed some that were sick were not only human but also supes. How did they get sick?

There was a Lycan there who looked like he'd seen better days, but as he and his group of sick individuals approached me, green spit leaked from their mouths. I placed my hand on the ground forcing myself up as I held my other hand over my belly. No one would hurt a Helson. I was one and so was my unborn child.

"She smells delicious, and she's clean," Dirty Lycan said. He couldn't fully shift. He was stuck in half human, half Lycan form.

"I'll kill you before you touch me," I threatened. This wasn't the time to be terrified.

As the Lycan charged me with his group, I lifted my arms to the side throwing my head back as my flames grew. I didn't think I could do this, but when I faced the Lycan, he caught on fire. I was shocked, but I had no time to think about what I just did. My flames weren't the bright orange and yellow anymore, no now, I was burning dark blue. I couldn't think about anything else as I set the rest of them on fire. Then, I turned and ran for my life. I had to protect my baby. This baby was all that I had left of Xáne.

Chapter 4
Xánur

My phone rang, and the sound was deafening. I turned to my left reaching out blindly for my phone on the nightstand. I answered without checking who it was, "Helson."

"Get over here!" Asar's voice blared almost damaging my damn ear.

This woke me up as I opened my eyes and sat up on the bed.

"What is it?" I asked as I stood quickly slipping on a shirt and sweats.

"It's Cin," her name stopped me in my tracks.

I sighed running a hand through my hair. I shut my eyes trying to feel her through our tether, but something was wrong. Something was blocking it.

"Where is she?" My heart was beating a mile a minute. "Don't tell me, she left again." My voice deflated, even though, I tried to mask the hurt.

"No! You imbecile! Get over here. She's burning my entire house down, and I can't get to her. It's too hot. She's different, and she won't wake up!"

I didn't hear anything else past that as I made my way over to Asar's house. I didn't even think to take my car as I jumped out of my window letting my wings guide me to where she was.

I can't lose her, was all I could think about.

****

When I got closer, no one could miss that fire. Asar's entire house was on fire, yet it wasn't burning. This wasn't the normal color for flames. No, all of these ones were dark blue. Something changed her flames.

I landed next to Asar who stood in front of his house with other sentinels trying to put it out, but nothing was working.

"Stop!" I yelled. I glanced at Asar, "I can stop her. Don't worry old man." I gave him a reassuring smile. He looked like he had aged, and I knew it was because he was worried about Cin.

I took a deep breath as I made my way into his house. Asar had a loft like I did. We both bought out a whole building helping each other construct it all. I walked through the first layer of flames shifting to my true form with each step that I took. I didn't stop as I made my way up the stairs, going to the left towards the bedrooms. I stood right outside of her bedroom door. I turned the knob slowly opening the door and was met with an excruciating heat level. I didn't let that stop me as I made my way in there. I saw Cin laying on the bed clutching her belly and her head. Her mouth was open, yet no sounds came out.

"Cin?" I called out her name but nothing. "Cin," I called it out once more making my way to her bed, and she still didn't answer.

I sighed as I got in the bed with her. I turned her to face me. Her eyes were open, yet she couldn't see me. She was lost.

"Lucinda!" I yelled her name out once, and then, one more time. "You had better come back to me. I'm not done being mad at you dammit! Snap out of it!" My voice hit an all-time low. One that shocked even me.

Then, she blinked. *Fuck.* She blinked and came back into focus.

"Xáne..." She called out to me, and I never knew just how much I needed to hear that.

"Cin, I need you to call your flames back, you're safe. No one is going to hurt you."

Tears fell from her eyes as the flames dimmed but were still there.

"No!" She shrieked as she tried to move out of the hold I had her in. "Someone is after me. They hurt me and took away our baby forever. I have to find my baby, Xáne."

I was speechless. What could I say? I saw her memory; our baby was stillborn.

"Lucinda..." The tone in my voice must've triggered something because she began crying. Had she ever mourned for our baby?

"Oh Xáne, our little girl is dead, I'm so sorry. I should've told you. I shouldn't have left."

I hated seeing her cry. I pulled her into my arms enveloping her with my wings. Something was wrong, everything about this didn't make any sense. Her leaving without saying a word to me. Everything Cin did, she gave me a clue about, but why was it that when she left, she didn't say anything? Why had I never thought about that?

Was it my fault? Did I cause her to lose our daughter?

****

Lucinda

When I woke up, I didn't recognize where I was. This wasn't the room that I stayed in at Asar's place, or as he called it, our place. He was the best friend I didn't deserve but kept because I was selfish. I surveyed the room. It looked familiar, but the décor was different. When I glanced up at the ceiling, the giant, black Victorian mirror reminded me where I was. The longer I stared at my reflection, the more glimpses of memories I buried deep inside invaded my mind; the way I rode Xáne reverse cowgirl, I would watch from the mirrors following his hands as they caressed my breasts and my midsection. Then, when I gazed into his eyes, he would be staring right back at me. The intense look in his eyes would drive me crazy, and I wouldn't want to stop.

My thighs would be shamelessly pleading with me to stop, but I wouldn't. As long as those intense, pale blue eyes kept me captive, I'd keep going. The memories didn't stop there, no. The memories escaped out of my head venturing to my body. I felt Xáne's hands everywhere on my aching body. It's been so long since I've felt him on me, and the best part of it, the high that I'm always chasing for is when he... Oh God, when his fangs tear through the first layer of skin, then sink deep penetrating every layer and pushing me to a climax that I couldn't resist. Xáne was the only one who could snatch an orgasm from me with a touch. How did I stay away from him for so long?

"Cin..." He called my name out saying it as he needed me as his air to breathe.

My reflection was no longer of me waking up in his bed. Instead, it was of a memory. The raw scene of us not making love but fucking. The way he lapped up my blood with his tongue as his fingers worked my clit into overdrive. I always felt full with him and now as I came back to the reality as Xáne yanked me out of the memory.

My body still felt the aftereffects as I repeatedly blinked slowly sitting up. Xáne stood in front of me with a cocked eyebrow, his hair in a top knot, and a towel wrapped lowly around his waist. I couldn't stop my eyes as they perused his body. This man was an orgasm personified. The addition of the tattoos over his body made him that much sexier. Fuck me!

"Do I have to yank you out of another memory, Cin?" Xáne spoke.

If he'd just shut up, I would be able to concentrate and come back to the here and now. He wasn't helping.

Just then, I felt Asar as he slipped into my mind.

Don't go raping my cousin, now.

Xáne rolled his eyes as he turned away from me walking out of the room. Damn, his entire back had tattoos, too. He had angel wings and clouds that took over his entire back. This one was new to my eyes. It would be sexy to see from the mirror while my fingers perused his back as he slipped inside of me.

I'm still here.

Asar said, I felt him roll his eyes.

Sorry.

"You're not sorry," Asar chuckled as he came in the room wearing a suit.

I eyed him up and down. He had a custom fitted, all black suit with a crisp, white dress shirt and bowtie. He had his hair freely flowing. He strutted towards me with his hands in his pocket and a big smile on his face.

"You look sexy as fuck. Where are you going?"

"We, my dear, plus one are going to the annual royal dinner," he answered as if I should've known this a long time ago.

"Oh… but I'm not part of the royal families."

Asar gave me his million-dollar smile.

"You are and will always be part of the royal family. Now," He gestured to the bathroom with his head. "Your dress is in there. Go get ready. You still know how to do your make-up... right?"

"I went to the other side, not fucking mars, bro. Plus, this isn't my house anymore. I don't have any of my stuff here."

Asar had the nerve to shake his head at me, "Did you also lose your entire brain there? You really think this isn't your home? Open your eyes, Cin... that stubborn-ass cousin of mine has never moved on even if he thinks he has. Now, I'd like it if you'd hurry your ass up so that you can braid my hair down like you used to."

I kissed my teeth, getting out of bed making my way to the bathroom. I glanced at Asar before heading in there, "Thank you for taking care and watching over him while I wasn't here."

He placed his hand over his heart and bowed like a fool with his eyes holding my gaze, "I will always watch over the both of you, my Queen," he grinned. "Even if the King thinks he can do it all by HIMSELF!" He yelled out the last part as if Xáne couldn't hear him to begin with.

I chuckled blowing him a kiss.

"Oh, you spoil me too much." He acted as if he caught it with his hand.

"HURRY UP!" Xáne yelled from wherever he was in the house.

Asar winked at me as he left with a mischievous grin on his face. He was too much.

Chapter 5
Xánur

I left earlier than Asar and Cin, I needed some air. Plus, no one was expecting me to walk in with her, and I needed to keep my space. It was getting harder not to touch her. Her scent of brimstone and cinnamon enveloped me all over whether I liked it or not. I couldn't get rid of it anymore, and the first time it took me a year and a half just to not have my body react to that scent alone. If my nose got a whiff of it, my wings would threaten to free themselves so that they could fly out to wherever to find her.

Losing Cin was the hardest thing I had ever faced. Wars, killing, and even when I took over as the king, none of that was hard for me, but her not being there when I woke up that morning, it changed my life. I searched everywhere for her. I crossed to the other side of the world looking for her not caring about anything. I knew I wouldn't die or catch the virus so that first year I searched for her, yet she didn't turn up. I thought she died at first or that someone took her, but the tether though barely felt, made me know she was alive. I searched throughout our side of the world, as well, going from house to house looking for her, but then, it all became clear. That night when I made love to her, her flames burned me from head to toe. She knew that it would take twice as long for me to wake or heal, so she left then.

I felt a hand cover my right one as I stared out of the window of the limo. I turned, staring down at Jaya's hand over mine. She was beautiful to me, a great friend and partner, but I would never be able to love her. Cin had every part of my heart, and I didn't know how to take it back from her without killing myself in the process.

"We're here, Xáne," I cringed at the nickname.

"I told you not to call me that."

"But she calls you that, why can't I?"

"Because I hate her and the nickname. I don't want to hear it. I've gone three years without hearing it, and I don't want to hear it again. Please." I stepped out of the limo as the valet opened it.

I should've known Jaya wouldn't have dropped it. Lately, all she did was try to argue with me comparing shit to Cin. It wasn't helping the cause nor making me feel like I wanted to be with her. I got with Jaya because she didn't remind me of Cin. I wanted a fresh start. She came up to my side slipping her hand into my arm, "Just give me something, Xánur," she demanded.

I glanced down at her. I knew my eyes had shifted from the reflection in hers, "I am your King, and you will do right not to press me about this shit again. Am I understood?"

Jaya cleared her throat, straightening her back as she sharply nodded.

We walked into Vali's home away from the Kingdom. He liked to live lavishly, so he bought this mansion trying to one-up me, why? I don't know.

****

Asar and Cin showed up half an hour later as cocktail hour was almost over. I sensed her before she even stepped into the room, and when she did come into the grand hall where we were chit-chatting, the other royals gasped. I took a deep breath slowly turning towards her. When my eyes landed on them, all I could do was blink.

"Is she serious?" I heard Jaya whisper to me, but nothing registered as Cin looked like a fucking goddess.

She stole my breath away as she came in with an all-black, diamond embroidered, see-through gown that was off the shoulders. The diamonds covered her nipples perfectly, along with her pussy, but her legs could be seen through the material. She wore all black heels. I eyed her from her feet to her face. Fuck! My dick knew what it wanted more than anything else in the world. The material that covered the train covered everything else from her waist down in the back. The way the material held up her breasts made them appear so damn delectable. They were definitely bigger than I remember.

Her hair was up in a messy bun making me want to pull it out and fuck her up against the wall. Her face was perfect from the natural look to whatever lipstick she put on her lips. My dick craved to slip in between them. My entire body shuddered at seeing her like this.

Down boy! Asar's voice slipped in my head.

It took me forever to take my eyes off her, but when I finally did, I narrowed my eyes at Asar. This was his doing. He smirked at me, winking like he didn't have a care in the world.

I will kill you. I said to him.

He smiled this time, showing all his stupid ass teeth. I lowly growled taking a step towards them. I didn't like how they were all looking at her, and Asar just had to make it worse by slipping his hand on her back leading her away from me.

A hand on my chest stopped me from advancing towards them, I looked down to see Jaya in front of me.

"What?" I asked.

She was pissed.

"You forget that she left you… right? Not the other way around!" She whispered harshly.

She didn't get it; my dick didn't care if she left me as long as she was wearing that damn dress. The same dress I forbid her to wear when she bought it for the first fucking time. My upper lip twitched as I tried to restrain myself.

I leaned in as if I was going to kiss Jaya, and then, I went towards her ear, not wanting to embarrass her.

"Don't ever fucking tell me what she did or didn't do. I know all too well who she left. Don't push me, Jaya." I shouldn't have taken my frustrations out on her, but she was doing too much right now.

I walked away needing a drink before I did something reckless like teleport in front of Cin and fuck her on the dining room table in front of everyone. I cracked my neck as I reached the bar on the far end of the room.

"Give me something strong," I told the bartender.

"A vampire king needing alcohol is unheard of," I knew that damn voice from anywhere.

I turned to my right, "Don't you have some duties to be fulfilling right now, Vali?" I eyed him up and down. His auburn hair was gelled back out of his face, and his green eyes shined bringing more awareness to his freckles. He wore a smoky gray suit, a crisp white dress shirt, and a bow tie.

"I do, but my... my... " He paused for dramatic effect. He was always so damn dramatic. As he paused, I got my drink and chugged it all in one go. "She's looking exquisite, doesn't she? She's filled out much more than before."

I side eyed him before I fully turned my body to see who he was looking at. He was gawking at Cin as if she was a treat brought for him.

"And she came in, like a true queen to a Vampire King. She looks delectable, just imagine the things you could do with those curves," Vali could never shut up. "You're a greedy one, King. You can't have the main course and dessert. You have to give one up for the other, and I vote on giving up the main course because I'm quite famished."

By his last words, I knew my eyes had shifted once more. I placed my empty glass down on the bar not realizing that I had crushed it. Then, I stood in front of Vali blocking his sight of Cin. I cleaned off some imaginary lint from his suit leaving trails of the blood from my wound. I fixed his bow tie making it tighter messing with his circulation. I glared at him letting him know what wasn't about to happen,

"If you so much as lay a finger on her in any way, I will cut your dick off and feed it to you. She is not your main course or anyone else's. She will always be mine. Do I make myself clear, temporary King Vali?"

I could tell he wasn't sure if I would take his head off in front of the other royals, but he clearly didn't know me well enough. I would if he pushed.

"You'd lay waste to your people for her?" His voice strained.

"I'd lay waste to the world for her." The severity of my words shook even me.

Let him go. He won't touch her.

Asar's voice slipped in my mind. I let Vali go with a scowl, and I walked off needing air before I changed my mind.

****

Lucinda

I watched as Xáne made his way out of the room. Asar made a move to go after him, but I placed my hand on his chest.

"Let me go after him. I think it's time him and I talk. It sucks that it has to be here but better than anywhere else."

Asar nodded.

"Take the elevator to the third floor, he's there. He knows the room is spelled so no one can hear him rage but you and I, Cin. We can feel it."

I nodded as I turned away to leave, but Asar's hand stopped me. I looked at him, "What is it?"

Asar sighed, and for the first time since I came back, I saw the worry in his eyes.

"Don't break his heart again, Cin. I love you, I really do but that's my brother you hurt. I know he's too stubborn to admit it to you, but he really wants to know why you left the way you did. He searched for you, Cin, and I went with him. You didn't see his breakdown, I did so if you're going up there to break his heart all over again, leave and don't come back this time."

Tears welled up in my eyes. I knew what Asar was saying, and I understood him. This was his family that I hurt. I know he loved me and that's why he forgave me.

"I promise, I won't ever break his heart again. He's my everything, Asar. He really is," I confessed.

"Then, act like it," Asar said. Then, he smiled like a kid in the candy store. I really loved this man. He was my family.

I winked at Asar as I made my way towards the elevator. I took a deep breath knowing that what I was about to do was scary, and I needed to say it even if he pretended like he didn't want to know.

****

When I got to the third floor, I could feel the invisible barrier. It was strong, and as I took another step off the elevator, I hit an invisible wall. Xáne had to let me come in.

"Xáne... " I called out to him, but there was no reply. "I want to talk, and after I say what I have to say, if you still don't want me around, then I will go but please, let me put your heart back together."

It was silent for so long, and I sighed. He didn't want to hear it. I failed not only Xáne but Asar too. Just as I was about to turn away, I was pulled in through the barrier.

I took in the room. It was big enough to be a ballroom, except, there were no decorations. It was just empty as hell. I searched for Xáne, and I found him out on the balcony looking at the night sky. He was so gorgeous tonight with his all-black suit, black dress shirt, and skinny black tie. His hair was up in that top-knot showcasing the hell out of his eyes. I should've told him that he looked handsome tonight, but I was being a coward.

I walked over to him, "Can I join you?" I asked him. Xáne didn't say anything, but he shrugged his shoulders. I smiled as I walked out joining him.

We stood there admiring how beautiful and quiet the night was. There was so much turmoil going on with me, and I was damn nervous. How was I going to start, and what was I going to say to this man? To my husband and father of our deceased child? I deeply inhaled and then exhaled, "I'm sorry Xáne... I, I wish I could've told you. I didn't mean to break your heart or anything. What I did was selfish and stu-," He cut me off.

"Why didn't you tell me? I would've made sure to go with you. I could've protected you. You still could've had our dau-." Shit, he couldn't even bring himself to say it.

Xáne snatched the hair tie off and ran a hand through his scalp. He was frustrated. He didn't know how to convey his feelings properly. I knew this too well. I didn't need the tether or his mind to tell me that. It was all in the way that I knew him.

"You wanted to protect me just like how I wanted to protect you," I admitted.

This statement caused Xáne to turn around to face me abruptly. He was angry. So much angrier than I knew.

"You wanted to protect me, Cin? From what? Don't speak to me about protection. I didn't even know that my own wife ran away from me in the middle of the night, and she was pregnant! PREGNANT! Cin!" The tears threatened to escape from his eyes as well. "I let you, the most important person in my life, slip through my fingers, and I caused you to lose our child. I lost that child right along with you even before I could rejoice in the thoughts of bringing her to the world. You robbed me of that, Lucinda."

Xáne put his hands up in surrender sniffing as he was trying hard not to cry for the loss of our child. He glanced at the night sky again, and then, he turned away from me. He wanted to walk away, but I wasn't going to let him. As he walked back into the ballroom, I followed him and yelled out.

"I wanted to find my parents!" At that statement, he stopped in his tracks. "What kind of a Queen would I be to you if I didn't even know who I was? People talked about me. They said I didn't know who I truly was and that using my powers wouldn't benefit them. I needed to find them so that I could be the queen you deserve! Dammit, Xánur! Why are you so fucking clueless!" I shouted at his back.

He turned around with fury in his eyes.

"I'm fucking clueless?" He marched up to me as I stood in the middle of the ballroom. "How fucking dare you? All you had to do was ask, Cin, and I would've sent men with you to find your parents if you wanted to do it alone. Asar could've protected you and our child. All I wanted was you. I didn't care what anyone said about you because you were my mate, my everything, my goddamn reason for breathing! I would've found your parents for you! Did you not understand how much I loved you? How much I fucking love you?"

Xáne and I had our fights before, but this was the first time he was ever this up close to my face and this angry, yet my body loved it. I wanted to concentrate on everything and just have him forgive me, but my eyes went to his lips. The way they moved when he talked, the vein on his neck, and the intensity of his eyes on me.

"I'm so sorry about our child, Xáne. I am. You have to know I would never have gone had I known. I loved you way too much to have ever hurt you in that way. Shit, I still love you way too much for my own good. You are my everything, my husband, and my mate. I can never separate from you, and you have to believe me that even though I wanted to search for my parents, I would've left you a note or something. I can't remember why I didn't. Every time I try to remember, I get headaches, and something blocks it."

"Something like what? Headaches? How intense?" I almost broke out into a smile, this was my husband that I remembered. He cared about me in every way.

Xáne must've noticed because he cleared his throat. He turned away from me as he always did so that he could collect all his emotions, but I took this opportunity to touch his back. I exhaled when he didn't push my small hand away, so I seized this opportunity as I slipped my arms around him and hugged him like I used to. The tears that I tried my best not to let out, slipped without my consent. I couldn't stop them as they flowed. I laid my forehead on his back, and he flexed it.

"Lucinda… " He called out to me, and it made me sob harder. I missed him so damn much. "Please don't cry, love. You know I can't handle it when you cry. I told you I would never be the reason why you cried."

As he said this, he removed my arms from around him and turned to face me. Xáne pulled me into his arms letting me cry not caring if I ruined his clothes. My heart ached at the first proper contact I've had with him since I've been back. I hugged him so tight while breathing him in. I never wanted to let him go.

"I missed you so much, Xáne. So damn much, you have no idea how it was out there without you. I couldn't even feel you, and it tore at my heart. Just forgive me, please?"

"I missed you too, Cin. It'll take some time, but let's start over." He pulled me out of his arms making me look up at him.

I gave him a small smile as he wiped my tears out of my face. I sniffled, stretching my hand out, "Hi, my name is Lucinda Howell, and I'd like to be your friend if you'll have me," I boldly said, even though, that wasn't what I wanted. I knew this was going to take time.

Xáne smiled, and my world crashed and burned.

"Hi, Lucinda Helson, I'm your husband, Xánur Helson, but I don't mind being your friend… for now."

Only Xáne could make me feel like I was floating on a thousand clouds for granting me a smile, a handshake, and letting me know that he was my husband even if we were only friends when it came to our relationship status.

Chapter 6
Xánur

My name is Lucinda Howell, and I'd like to be your friend if you'll have me...

She wasn't serious. I couldn't wipe the smile off my face after that. When we made our way back to the dinner, everyone was getting ready to eat. Not even Vali's antics of having Cin sit by his side could take this feeling away from me. The food was served, and everyone began having conversations. I looked down at my food. It was veal, and I scowled hating the way it tasted. This was not my favorite thing to eat, I'd rather starve. Before I could complain or say anything else, one of the servers took the plate and replaced it with a well-done steak, veggies, and potatoes. Then, he filled my glass with red wine. I cocked an eyebrow and glanced at Cin who sat on the opposite end on the left side of him.

You're welcome. She winked at me.

I really did miss her like crazy, and my mind began pondering on what she said. Every time she tried to remember what happened to her, she got headaches, and I wanted to know about her trip. How did she survive it all out there and what made her come back?

I want to talk to you after this. I said to her.

What did I do this time? She rolled her eyes as she sipped her white wine.

First, that dress... I'm burning it. I glared at her.

Cin choked on her wine coughing as Asar, who sat by her, quietly chuckled lightly patting her on her back.

You do know I'm not yours, right? Aww. It was cute, she was trying to establish boundaries.

As long as I'm living and breathing, you will always be my wife, my mate, and mine all around. What did she think this was?

Did she really think this friendship shit was going to work? I warned her not to touch me, but she made the mistake of wrapping her arms around me. She woke the devil up again, and this time, there was no taming me.

Vali started clinking his glass wanting attention as always. I eyed him for a moment as he stood up wanting to talk, but then, I turned my focus back on Cin who shied away from my gaze.

"So, this year's dinner is one of importance. Our queen, Lucinda Helson is back. Although we may not know how or why you disappeared, we are glad to have you back. We will be hosting a proper welcoming party for you once you've settled in if that's alright with you and the Vampire King? He's still your husband… correct?"

I took another sip of my drink slowly not caring about what Vali was saying. I cocked my eyebrow at Vali as he stared at me with a challenging look in his eyes.

"Yes," Cin responded. "I am his wife, and he is my husband. That will never change." The challenging tone in her voice made me turn my attention on her. Cin was staring right at Jaya. She continued, "Just like how others think they've taken my place while I was gone…" Oh, shit. She turned her focus back on Vali with a mischievous smile, "Is the same way you, King Vali are currently abusing your title and position. Don't question my husband or me on our status again and behave accordingly. I am your queen and he, my husband, is your true King."

If I could kiss this woman right now, I would.

"Spoken like a queen," Vali just had to have the last word as he took his seat.

And you think we could only be friends with the way you're ready to snap Jaya's neck huh, baby? I bit my bottom lip as I caressed her neck through our tether.

Cin sat up straight trying to pretend she didn't feel a damn thing, and I knew this friendship wasn't going to last more than two weeks whether she liked it or not.

You keep caressing me like that, and I'll burn you.

This time, I laughed out loud, and I knew it shocked everyone around me. I hadn't laughed like this in so long.

"Xánur, are you okay?" Jaya whispered.

I nodded. I didn't give a damn if they all thought I was weird.

Oh, I'd like to see you burn me Cin... You shouldn't have worn that dress.

I couldn't take my eyes off her.

We're friends remember? She tried to remind me. *Plus, you have a girlfriend.* She smirked.

I can change that in a heartbeat if you'd like. Were we flirting?

Before she could reply, Asar interrupted.

Can you two stop flirting with me here? You could both do this on a different frequency. Fucking weirdos.

I shook my head staring at Cin, holding her gaze.

Now, now Asar. You know I can't be on that frequency with her unless she submits to me again and like she said, we're just friends. Have a good night, friend.

I stood knowing that Jaya would follow. As I turned my back on all of them walking out, through the tether, I conjured up the sensation of me licking Cin's clit once, twice, and then, I stopped it.

"Shit!" I heard her cuss as I left the house. My laughter echoed through the foyer of the house traveling all the way to her ears.

I may not have fully let it all go, but she fucked up. Cin shouldn't have established her position in my life, it was only going to turn me on.

****

Lucinda

As we left a little while after Xáne and Jaya, I couldn't regulate my body from what Xáne did. I didn't have his abilities, so I couldn't do what he did to me, but lord did I miss this. Xáne never had to physically touch me to get my entire body to feel like it was on fire and every time he did, I knew how everyone felt when they experienced being close to my flames. I shut my eyes as Asar drove us back home, but that didn't work as Xáne rich laughter filled my mind.

"I need you to turn it down a notch there Cin. You know I can smell your arousal. I'm not trying to get into an accident."

I shook my head.

"I can't. Your stupid ass cousin has no shame doing this to me."

Asar laughed, "It's like you forgot how he was. He's always been like this, Cin," then Asar stopped in front of Xáne's house. "Cin, what the hell is going on with you? It's like you remember things but then don't."

I sighed. "I seriously don't know Asar. There are things that I know either I used to do or that Xáne did, but then, it's like every time he does them, it's a new experience for me. I feel like being out there made me forget some things. I saw so much out there, man. I don't even know how I survived."

Asar turned the ignition off.

"Come on, let's go inside and talk. I think it's time you tell both Xáne and me what you saw out there, and we get you checked."

"You think Xáne already knows something is off?" I asked.

"Yeah, when you guys came down the stairs from your talk, he told me that something was off about you. He mentioned the headaches. I already contacted the one doctor him and I trust."

Okay, was all I could say. I was exhausted. We exited out the car and went towards the house. Life, as I knew, was changing faster than it did the first time I met Xáne.

****

The smell of smoke filled my room. I woke up in shock hoping that I didn't set anything on fire. Asar's place wasn't damaged, but he had a lot of repairs to do so here him, and I were in Xáne's house. We each had our own room, and even though I craved to sleep in Xáne's arms, I wanted to give him some time to let the hate that he felt towards me dissipate.

When I opened my eyes, there wasn't a thing burning in my room. I sniffed the air again, turning towards the open window that the smoke was coming from. I jumped out of bed pulling back the covers to see what was going on and there Xáne's back profile was as he stood in front of a fire. I narrowed my eyes trying to see what it was, and then, it clicked. He was burning my DAMN dress! I didn't even think about a thing as I ran out of the room, turning left and heading down the stairs not stopping at all to see who was in the house. Had I stopped, I would've noticed Jaya who was sitting on the couch, but I didn't as I yanked the back door open.

"What the fuck do you think you're doing? Xáne?" I didn't care that I was barefoot on the grass.

I stopped in front of the metal trashcan as I gasped out loud. My dress was burning, all of it. This wasn't normal fire, I knew it because the diamonds seemed to burn with the rest of the dress.

"I told you never to wear this dress, didn't I? And I told you I'd burn it the moment it caressed your body as my hands did. Did you think I forgot what I said to you before?" Xáne was insane.

I glared up at him as he eyed me. He was staring again, doing that thing where he doesn't take his eyes off me until I turn away, but today, I was pissed. I would keep eyeing him until he submitted to me.

Xáne smiled as he stepped closer to me,

"You want to fight me, don't you? Mmmm, swing, Cin." I wasn't even thinking as I formed a fist and swung.

Xáne could've ducked, yet he didn't. He let me punch him in the face, and all he did was grin like a madman as he checked his jaw.

"Fuck! You could've ducked!" I exclaimed.

"I know, but you wanted to hit me, so I let you. It'll never happen again but know this, if you wear another dress like this one, I'll burn that too with no problem at all."

"You're crazy! Dude, that was uncalled for. I could've just admired it from afar. You psycho!" I shrieked like a damn banshee.

All Xáne did was laugh further proving my point. He waited until I calmed down before he lowered his body picking me up and placing me over his shoulder. Oh, hell no!

"I swear on everything I love, Xáne, if you don't put me down, I'll really burn you," and I was serious.

Xáne continued to laugh as he walked into the house not heeding my words.

"You'll just go back for that dress, and we have to talk anyway. I made coffee, you still like that, right?"

"What the hell have you done with angry Xáne and who the hell are you?"

"Oh darling, I'm still mad, but I chose to go about it differently. You see, me being angry at you isn't going to make this friendship work, now will it?"

I rolled my eyes ready to knock his ass out, and then, I spotted Jaya as Xáne turned the corner towards the kitchen.

Your girlfriend is here... put me down! I communicated telepathically.

She's not my girlfriend. Xáne responded. *She's here as one of the sentinels. I need her to check something.*

So, what? You just broke up with her? Why? I was nosey.

Because you asked me to. Xáne answered nonchalantly.

No, I didn't.

Xáne didn't answer. Instead, I felt the tip of one of his talons as it left a trail of goosebumps down the back of my right thigh.

You're going to wish you didn't ask that of me. You wanted your husband back, and you've got him, Mrs. Helson.

What the hell had happened to the Xáne I left and who the hell was this dude?

Chapter 7
Xánur

When I got out of the shower, there Asar was sitting on my bed as if he was my woman. I narrowed my eyes, "Now, why the hell are you in here like this?"

"I needed to speak to you in a sealed room. No one can hear this, and I need you to block out Cin, too."

"Uhm, okay?"

I took me only a second to block her. She wouldn't notice right away, but the longer I blocked her, she'd start to feel it.

"What is it?" I asked Asar.

"It's father, he's taking a trip here with Uncle."

I shuddered. "Now, why the hell do our fathers want to make an appearance all of a sudden? We haven't seen them in eons."

"You know why they're coming, don't you?" Asar eyed me, and I turned away from him, walking towards my walk-in closet. He was still talking as I looked for something simple to put on. "The prophecy bro."

I rolled my eyes, "How could I ever forget?"

That prophecy haunted me much more when Cin came back.

Sons of brothers who aren't related by blood yet are closer than blood. One who can transform into another being... flames will consume you from head to toe bringing forth all parts of your lineage. Vampire Nephilims, twins but not by birth with wings and talons are altered into the biggest creature ever to rule. Fangs along with sharp teeth and paws with talons, each part of them shall be one.

The prophecy came true the night I made love to Cin, and she burned me inside out. As I was healing, she left me and as I healed, something happened.

I was in bed trying to force myself to heal as my mind woke up before I could open my eyes. I couldn't tell whether Cin was there with me or not because everything in me hurt. I didn't even know I was screaming my head off until I heard Asar yelling my name out, but by then, something was going on with my body.

The first cracking of my bones almost caused me to pass out, yet the healing reduced the pain. This happened to every bone in my body, and for the first time in my life, I wished that I was dead. After what felt like an eternity, I opened my eyes. I looked around, my vision was clearer than it had ever been before. Something else was going on, and I could feel it in the triple heartbeats in my chest. I went to touch my chest, but I rolled off the bed. I looked down at the floor, my gasp coming out as a whimper. I had fucking paws, I blinked a couple of times wishing that I was dreaming instead of whatever the fuck was happening.

"Xánur!" I heard Asar's voice, had he been calling me?

When I turned his way, I knew for a fact the prophecy came true because the moment, our eyes made contact, I knew that Asar was my twin and not by birth. He didn't even get a chance to speak as the transformation hit him too. I would have never believed it had I not witnessed it with my own two eyes. We were something the kingdom had never seen before, and we knew it.

It should've clicked that moment for me that something happened with Cin but as I recovered nothing made sense not even the fact that she was the flames that consumed me and triggered Asar and I's transformation.

I slipped on some black sweats, a black tee shirt and walked out to meet Asar. He was pacing back and forth, only he would be this worried,

"You know why they are coming. They want to make sure you haven't transformed, but we both know you have. It happened that night Cin burned you from head to toe, that's why it took you so long to go after her."

I ran a hand through my hair scratching my scalp as if that would help the situation.

"I know dammit! You don't have to remind me. How the hell would I know I would be a creature that has never existed.

The question here is who the fuck told father or Uncle? I love the two bastards, but if they know, then they are going to want to stay and run my life. I'm too old for that shit, and I am NOT fighting another battle for them. Ever!"

Asar nodded, "I know. The last damn part of the prophecy says the same shit. The protector turns into the same shit which we've both witnessed. Who said I wanted to be a damn Lycan and vampire along with being goddamn Magni's son!" Asar yelled, and it was my turn to look at him as though he had lost his mind. He took a deep breath and cleared his throat, "we've got to make sure those two psychos don't make it here or else, back to royal shit we don't care for."

"You don't have to tell me twice, now let's go talk to Cin and find out what happened to her. I have a feeling someone knew about this prophecy and tried to fuck it up. I wouldn't have cared to be something else, but I do care that they did something to her, and we lost our daughter because of it. I want to know who put the idea of wanting to find her parents in her head too, she never cared before." I thought about a lot yesterday.

"I can tell that someone messed with her mind or her memories rather. There are things she doesn't remember even from before. I noticed when we were coming back from dinner. I'll get into contact with some folks and see what I can find out."

I smirked at Asar, "When I find who did it, they will have hell to pay. I haven't tortured a soul in so long."

"Neither have I and speaking of dumbasses, why is your ex downstairs with your wife?"

If I weren't so invested in hearing what happened with Cin, I would fight Asar, and he knew it.

"Please, don't make me mess your ugly-ass face up some more."

Asar laughed as he stood walking towards my bedroom door. He opened the door walking out and just had to be even more annoying,

"Jesus, Xáne! I'm your cousin, stop trying to get with me. I told you I don't want you, but if you give me Cin, I promise to let you kiss my cheek."

"I hate you so damn much Asar, I should bash your face in right now." I teleported in back of him and punched him hard in the back.

Asar fell to the ground from the impact and because he was caught off guard. He laughed hard as he vanished. I knew he teleported to where Cin was because I felt the moment the shock registered that he had spooked her.

Only Asar could have a serious conversation with me and make me want to knock his ass out in the next breath. This was what family was for anyways.

****

I stared at Cin waiting for her to start talking, well, we all were. Asar sat in his sweats and tee across from me with Cin next to him. Jaya sat on the left side of me on the ottoman wearing her all black sentinel uniform. She kept looking at me as though I had a solution for her, but I didn't. I told her yesterday that I couldn't be with her and had she not flipped out, I would've thought she was nuttier than she already was, so I let her throw her weak punches and then I told her ass to get the fuck out. Jaya thought I didn't see the way she looked at Cin, she envied her, but there was nothing I could do to change how much I loved Cin even if I wasn't with her at the moment. I wasn't a cheater so there was no way I was going to have both of them plus it wouldn't have been fair.

I didn't want to hurt Jaya of course, but if I even thought of hurting Cin, it would kill me. I could never make her cry because of me.

"Do I have to?" Cin glanced at Asar, and he nodded.

"Hey! Friend… " I called out to Cin knowing she was not going to like being referred to that, even though, she suggested it. When her eyes set on mine, she glared at me like she imagined killing me so many times in her mind.

"What, friend?" She gritted through her teeth, and I almost laughed in her face.

I cleared my throat, "I'd really like to hear about how you did out there and how you survived and all of that."

Cin side eyed Jaya, then she looked back at me, "Does she need to be here for it?"

"Not if you don't want her to," I answered without much thought.

I took in Cin's appearance. She seemed like she went through a lot and didn't want to say it out loud, so I did what she asked of me. I faced Jaya, "You've got to go."

Jaya had the nerve to be offended.

"Are you serious right now? You called me over here!" She raised her voice.

"I did, and now, you've got to go," I glared at her. "Go do your job."

Jaya stood taking her exit. I faced Cin, "Come here, baby," I didn't wait for her to come to me as I teleported her to me.

Cin's face was priceless as she stared at me, bug-eyed.

"What the fuck was that?" She was either fascinated or scared. I wasn't sure which one yet.

"That's a story for another day... right now, we have to see what happened. Since you don't want to talk, I have no choice but to get the memories another way."

"What wa-?" Before she could finish her sentence, I pulled her in for a kiss. There were other ways that I could've gotten to her memories, but this was the way that I felt most pleased to do it.

Cin gasped granting my access to both her tongue and her mind; all three of us, Asar, Cin, and I were in her memories.

****

Lucinda

I couldn't think straight when Xáne kissed me. This wasn't the same as it was before, and I should've known. When he kissed me, a fire buried so deep within me ignited traveling and spreading throughout my body. If I thought I was hooked on him before then now, I was obsessed. I leaned into his kiss letting him devour me as I wrapped my arms around his neck straddling him in the process.

The deeper the kiss, the more my memories were conjured up. I was lost in him as it took over.

I was running after I escaped through the wall. Someone watched my back, a woman, but I couldn't remember who. She was helping me, and she called herself a friend. I met her before this but where? I couldn't remember. My breath hitched, I stopped for a moment feeling Xáne's tether, something was wrong. I turned around to go back, but a voice spoke so loud, "Keep going! Don't look back!"

I cried out feeling myself being turned away from Xáne. It hurt so bad to leave, my body was physically shaking.

"It'll wear off! Just keep going."

I was sweating bullets by the time that I made it far enough that I couldn't tell where the border or the invisible wall was.

"Xáne… " I whispered not able to hold it in anymore. I dropped to my knees on the dirty ground ruining my all black attire, crying my heart out as if I buried him. My fingers itched to touch him again. I couldn't stop the tremors that broke out through my entire body.

I wanted to feel him through our tether, but something prevented that, and then, it was as if someone struck me on my back. I cried out dropping to the ground clutching my head as pain so excruciating took over. I have never had anyone else in my head but Xáne and Asar, and they were gentle hums, but this one wasn't. This felt like someone was plucking pieces of my mind apart, someone that didn't have a physicality to it yet, it was being ripped apart, and I felt it all. Sounds of agony escaped my mouth as my flames changed colors. I didn't know before, but I knew now that it was because I left Xáne that the orange in my flames became blue.

My memories didn't go in chronological order. It was as if everything was jumbled up, but one memory that did not escape was the way that I protected our baby as I killed those Lycans.

It was as if I was walking Xáne and Asar down memory lane as they both held my hands. The next scene was gruesome as I woke up from being knocked out by an unknown person. I couldn't see their faces, but I knew there was more than one person. I cried out for my child wanting to protect it.

"No! No! Don't, please!" I begged, but they just stared at me as if I was speaking a foreign language.

A woman came in a face that I saw clearly. She wasn't sick nor puking those green things out of her mouth. She was healthy as ever; her brown skin shined brightly, her hair was braided down into two big braids, and she looked to be my age. I wondered what she was doing on this side, but I didn't get the chance to ask her that as I was hit with contractions again. She ran over to my side, holding my hand so tight and she whispered in my ear, telling me I would be okay. Then, she said something I never remembered… until now.

"No matter what, I will help you get out of here. You don't deserve to be here. I will make sure you and your baby get out."

"Hey!" the faceless man yelled at her, and she began shushing me and stroking my hair.

I could never forget her big brown eyes as they gazed into mine. She wasn't human, and I could tell by the way she was keeping my flames in check. What was she and why was she helping me?

****

That night was a night filled with regret as I lost my daughter because she wasn't breathing. I didn't stay awake after I passed out from carrying my daughter in my arms. When I came to, the same girl was dressing me up.

"Hey! Hey!" She whispered harshly. I wanted to stay awake, but I was slipping again. She slapped me hard, and that woke me up. Her eyes that once were brown now resembled an ocean. "You need to go! I'll take you away from here but don't come back. Go as far as you can! Escape for the both of us!"

I slowly got up not sure what she was talking about, but I was going to do as she asked.

"Why are you helping me?" I asked her as she led me out watching her back the entire time.

"Because you call his name in your sleep. You've been doing so for months, go back to him." I turned to look at her, and she had unshed tears in her eyes. She'd lost something. I could tell.

"What's your name?" I asked her.

"Hina," her soft voice replied to me.

"Like the great Nephilim, the moon goddess? The one we read about in books?"

She looked at me with a sad smile on her face.

"Yes. My mother was a great woman. She's gone, and this is why I am here. Get out before they find out you are one of a kind as well."

"Is that how you knew what I was?" I asked her as she led me towards a dead-end, but we crossed through it.

"Yes, now go… " I began to walk away from her slowly. "Wait!" She called me back, "If you had a son, what would you name him?"

"A son?" I tilted my head.

She nodded, rubbing her belly as if she was pregnant. I tried to keep my sadness to myself as I felt tears escape my eyes, "I'd name him Ezra but spell it E-x-r-a in remembrance of his father."

She smiled at me, "Exra… that's beautiful. I will take care of Exra and return him to his rightful owner."

I didn't get what she was talking about. Thinking that maybe they had driven her crazy, but she wasn't that crazy because she helped me escape. When I left, I roamed the dying side of the earth, fighting, killing, and looking for my parents. I never found them, and after three miserable years, my heart yearned too much for Xáne. It was as if my heart began beating for him not understanding why I was so far from him again. So, I trekked my way back to him hoping he'd have me back because I didn't understand why I left to begin with.

Chapter 8
Xánur

When I stopped kissing Cin, my body shook. I was angry as we slipped out of her memories and came back to our reality. I sat back on the couch with her still straddling me, none of this made sense and yet made all the sense in the world. I should've known that there was no way Cin would've willingly left me like that, but then again, what was this going to prove? What was all this meant to be about? Was she not supposed to come back? So many questions were swimming in my head, and I couldn't get a grip to answer any of them.

I felt Cin's hands on my face as she made me focus on her. I looked at her, but I couldn't see past my anger or her memories. I was so mad at myself for not seeing it, not feeling how she felt when she left and on top of that, I moved on from her. I chose to stop searching for her. I did this to us. If I had found her sooner, she wouldn't have gone through all of that.

"Hey," she tried to get my attention, but I avoided her eyes. I was ashamed of myself.

Asar stood, "I'll give you guys a minute. I'm going to clear my head, and I'll be back to talk about it all."

When Asar teleported out of the house, Cin was still trying to make me look at her, yet I couldn't.

"Baby… " she called out to me. I shook my head. "Look at me."

"I can't love. I really," I sighed my hands forming fists. "I can't fucking believe I gave up on you like that, and I blamed you for shit you didn't even do on purpose. How the fuck could I be so stupid!" I didn't even know where the rage was coming from, but I had to calm down.

I didn't even have time to think as Cin slapped the shit out of me.

I was in shock as she spoke, "I don't care, Xánur! None of that matters anymore! Don't you get it, baby? Now, you can't be mad at me anymore, and you can hold me like you used to. I'm not even mad that you tried, emphasis on the tried to move on, even if the bitch looks like she has brass balls."

She cocked her eyebrow at me, "Open your big ass ears and hear me well, nothing matters anymore except finding our son, you hear me? As long as you and I are okay, I don't care about anything that happened during those three years. Granted, I'm going to still kick that Amazonian bitch's ass for talking reckless, but for now, I want a hug, Xáne. Please, just love me."

I gazed into those eyes that I loved so damn much before pulling Cin into the tightest hug ever. I've loved her since I could last remember, and I was glad that the love never actually stopped because had it stopped, then I wouldn't be here with her again. I kissed her neck loving the feel of her skin on my lips. I've missed this for too long.

"Did you just slap me?" I asked her as I wrapped my arms tighter around her.

Cin had the nerve to giggle.

"Yeah, sorry, baby."

I sighed as I buried my nose into her neck. AHH, cinnamon and brimstone.

"Say it again."

"Baby."

"I thought I'd die without hearing that come from your lips. I love you Lucinda Helson."

I felt her lips on my shoulder, "I love you, too. Now, let's call Asar back so that we can talk about what to do with these headaches, the bastard who made me leave, and where Hina and my son are."

"You mean where Hina and our son are right? I still can't believe we have a surviving child. That means you were pregnant with twins, but because you passed out, you didn't see the birth of the second one," my chest swelled with pride. "Exra Helson."

We need you to come back Asar, we've got people to hunt and kill... and we need to find our family.

I communicated to Asar. I knew he was flying, and I felt him smile.

I can't believe I have a nephew and when we do find those responsible, let me rip them to shreds. It's been so long since I've last ripped someone's lungs through their throat.

I found myself smiling and not because I was happy. No, I was smiling because I knew that whoever was responsible for the loss of my wife, my daughter, and the disappearance of my son had hell to pay, and since I was a Helson, it only served right that I, the son of death, ripped their souls from their body. It was never too late to go back to my old ways of torturing a soul, instead of the body they inhibited in.

****

Lucinda

Asar was livid. Usually, he kept his emotions in check even around Xáne and I, but we both could tell that seeing everything that I went through had made him mad as hell. He sat there across from Xáne and me fuming like he needed to punch something or else he'd target either of us in the room. I had seen Asar pissed off before, and it was a scary sight. I needed Asar to calm down because if he didn't, then he was going to fuel Xáne to be on his level, and that was a bad combination. If ever I wanted to see our side of the world blow up, all I had to do was piss Asar off long enough for it to transfer over to Xáne, and when that happened, together they'd lay waste to it all. I was sure each of them could do it on their own, but the sick smiles they had on their faces when they were doing something mischievous still made me shudder till this day.

"Asar," I got off the couch and made my way to him. I kneeled in front of him waiting for him to look my way. "I'm going to need you to look at me before I smack the dog shit out of you like I did Xáne." I joked.

That got him to crack a smile as he now met my gaze, "I think the whole world heard it," Asar glanced at Xáne and then back at me. "You know I've always imagined you on your knees like this before me."

I knew what Xáne was going to do before I turned around. I ducked so fast as Xáne's fist swung. Shit! Asar's mood was worse than I thought. The impact of the punch caused the back of Asar's head to leave a big dent in the wall.

"Asar!" I yelled out.

"No!" He yelled back. He rolled his shoulders as he stood to face off Xáne.

I knew what he was doing. He was getting Xáne angrier instead of talking. Asar wasn't a talker, if he were in a rage, he would fight it out, and it was always with his cousin. These two were going to break everything in the house. I backed up, all the way to the corner of the living-room that I knew they weren't going to come near. They always seemed to know where I was, and they never got closer to me.

I watched in horror as Asar and Xáne threw punches at each other; Asar's fists sounded like thunder every time he connected with Xáne's jaw and Xáne's fists, well they were an anomaly. If ever there was a sound to what it felt like when your soul was being ripped out of your chest, then that was it. It was a scary sight to behold because two gigantic Nephilims were fighting. They had both transformed as their wings came to life; Asar's was the opposite of Xáne, his wings matched the color of Xáne's hair while Xáne's wings matched the color of Asar's. Asar had fangs and talons just like his cousin. I was so lost in the transformation that I almost missed the next moment.

Both Asar and Xáne continued to transform, and it scared the living shit out of me. As they fought knocking everything over, putting holes and dents into the wall, they became more than their true forms. They morphed into unspeakable beings. They were bigger about twice their vamp size in width. They didn't resemble regular Lycans who could stand on their hind legs. No, these big bastards were on all four like werewolves. I gasped, werewolves were extinct. They were legends, beings that were part of the stories grandparents passed down. It's been centuries since they became extinct, so what the fuck was this? My body shook as I tried to stand. I pressed my back on the wall knowing there was nowhere else to go.

As if sensing my fear, two pairs of eyes were set on me. They had stopped fighting and were now staring straight at me. They even had the snouts. If I weren't so terrified, I'd say that they were beautiful. Asar with the dirty blonde fur and Xáne with the midnight black fur.

"Guys… this shit isn't funny," they both growled at me, and I whimpered. I was scared shitless, and I felt tears running down my face.

I peered at Asar, who seemed to register who I was, and then, there was my husband. I looked at him. At this point I was crying like a maniac.

"Please," I pleaded as he took steps towards me that thundered through my chest. My heart dropped to my feet. "Xáne…" I called out to him, and then, he stopped not even a foot away from me.

We stared at each other. His eyes were huge and pale blue. He sat there and did the strangest thing ever, he bowed his head to me.

What the hell was going on?

Chapter 9
Xánur

I can't believe we shifted again, this time in front of Cin. I wanted her to find out but not like this. I wanted to be the first one to tell her about the prophecy and what it meant for us all, but of course, Asar was too damned pissed to talk about it. He wasn't much of a talker. He was more of a fighter, and he thinks I let him goad me into punching him, but he forgot I knew him. I smiled at him as I rubbed the ice pack on my shoulder that he had dislocated. He was worse than me because when he was in a rage, he never concentrated. He just threw hits like a mad man.

"What the fuck are you smiling about?" Asar threw his ice pack at me, and I caught it with my left hand.

I chuckled, shaking my head. "For someone who just got their ass handed to them, you seem to want to fight again."

He scowled, "If I weren't so mad, I'd definitely be a good match for you. We can't beat each other, dumbass," he stated.

"I'm just glad you've cleared your head even if you thought goading me with what you said to Cin was the reason."

He side-eyed me, "You knew?" He flinched when Cin wrapped the bandage around his torso tighter than she should've. "Jesus, Cin! Chill!"

Cin was pissed at the both of us. She was giving us the silent treatment and more to me than Asar as always.

"Shut up!" She exclaimed as she finished.

Usually, we healed faster, but because we attacked each other after we transformed, it took a day or two for us to heal fully. Cin moved away from Asar and came towards me. She was definitely not talking to me as she sat in front of me on the floor. I opened my legs wider, so she could come closer. She made sure the first-aid kit supplies she had were next to her as she began to apply some medicine that was made for slow healing cuts for supes. I stared at her as she ignored me focusing a little too much on the cuts on my face.

"You're seriously going to ignore me?" I knew she was going to, but it wouldn't hurt to ask.

Cin scowled, kissed her teeth, and pressed hard on the cut under my eye. The pain traveled all the way to my toes. I gritted my teeth trying not to let a sound out. I swear Cin was a sadist, and she just didn't realize it yet. As if she read my mind, she glared at me. I gave her my best boyish grin, and she narrowed her eyes at me. I almost had her. She stood, kicking me in the process as she left Asar and me in the disaster of the living room.

"So childish," I said as she made some noise and kept going wherever she was going.

Asar shook his head, "She must've been really scared."

I nodded as I jumped up to my feet, made my way to him, and offered him a hand. Asar took it and stood.

"Yeah, even right now, she's afraid of us. I can tell. I'm going to let her cool down so help me clean this shit up, since you wanted this to happen, asshole."

****

After we finished cleaning up the place, I knew a few tricks to get Cin to talk to me. She was finishing up in the shower. I took my sweats off remaining only in my black boxer-briefs. My shoulder would have to suffer a little as I reached out for the pull-up bar on the bedroom door. I heard every movement she made as I began doing pull-ups. I had to do a few before she came out so that she could see me sweating. I lost myself in the work out for a bit, and then, I heard the bathroom door open. I didn't look her way as I continued on with the task at hand. I could feel her eyes on me. The tether between us hummed so loud and vibrated through my entire body.

I glanced at Cin. She was doing exactly what I thought she was. Her eyes were stuck on my body as I continued doing the pull-ups. I did three more just to rile her up some more, and then, I stopped. I stood tall taking my sweet time as I walked by her making sure my arm brushed up on her wet skin. She shuddered. I was going to keep walking away, but I couldn't. I turned on my heel, wrapped my arm around her toweled body, and deeply inhaled.

"Mmmm," my tongue did its own thing as it licked a path from her shoulder all the way to her earlobe.

Cin moaned, and I broke.

I couldn't think straight as I made her face me. I yanked the towel from her body, and Cin smiled so brightly as if she was waiting for me to do that. She raised her eyebrow as if challenging me and waiting to see what I'd do.

"Are you going to apologize to your Queen, King Xánur?" And there it was. I was instantly hard.

I licked my lips and pulled my bottom lip into my mouth as I explored her body with my eyes. She was fucking beautiful from the scars to her size. She filled in some more when she came back, and I loved it. She wasn't small, so I knew I wasn't going to break her because she could take all of me.

I didn't even think about how I was going to apologize to her. I dropped to my knees as my lips made the first contact with her pussy lips. Cin was shocked, she thought I was going to tease her like I usually do, but no, this wasn't the time to tease. My hands gripped the back of her thighs as I lifted her up a bit, and my tongue licked her clit.

"Oh…" I could've laughed at her reaction, but I was too focused, and her arousal flooded my thoughts.

****

Lucinda

I should make Xáne apologize to me all the time. I wasn't afraid now like I was a while back when they transformed. At this moment, I was so lost in the way Xáne's tongue fucked me. How he managed to hit the right spots without so much as spreading my legs wide open was something I was glad to experience. Xáne teleported us to the bed as his tongue never lost focus. I felt my toes curl as he slid his fingers in my pussy. My arms reached out to hold on to whatever to keep me sane and try not to set myself on fire.

My flames itched to be set free, and my eyes were now fixed on that mirror. I watched as Xáne stole my soul through my pussy. The muscles in his back made this moment so much more. The tattoos on his back looked like they were animated. Xáne hooked his fingers, and I lost sight of myself as my flames came alive. They were pale blue now matching the color of Xáne's eyes. They enveloped us not consuming either one of us, and then, I couldn't see anymore as I felt it. I came so hard and strong that the tether between us caused Xáne to cum as well.

"Well shit… that's new," Xáne said as he panted trying to catch his breath.

Xáne got off the bed. I wanted to ask where he was going, but my body felt like it had just run miles all from him simply performing oral sex. I felt the bed dip as Xáne hovered over me. My body jolted a bit when I felt the cold cloth as he cleaned me up. Xáne wasn't watching what he was doing. Instead, he was staring into my eyes as he had always done before. His pale blue eyes were so beautiful to me, but the longer he stared, the more I wondered what the hell he was looking at.

"What?"

"Are you still afraid of me?" He asked with a serious expression on his face. "You know I would never hurt you, right? No matter what form I take. That's never going to happen."

"Is that why you bowed your head to me earlier?"

He nodded, some of his hair escaped the band he had secured it in.

"I wanted you to know that whatever form I take, I will always recognize you. You are my queen through and through, do you get that?"

I smiled, my heart melting at his words. "I get it."

He shook his head, "No, you don't. If it came down to me choosing you or my people, I will always choose you. I would die for you, Lucinda. Just promise me one thing?"

I couldn't help but gaze into his eyes the way he was just doing to mine a moment ago, "What's that Xánur?"

"Promise me that if ever someone utters how incompetent you are for me, you slice their throat because you are my other half. No one can tell you that you and I aren't it. They aren't us."

"I promise with all my heart, Xánur. I really do. Never again."

He gave me that boyish grin again as he leaned down and kissed me so passionately that I forgot all about the pain of not having him with me when I left. Xáne pulled away, and I whimpered. He chuckled as he gave me a couple of open mouth pecks.

"Rain check on this baby… right now, we have to go find who did this to you and find our son, so we can bring him back home."

I couldn't help the feeling that took over, "Our son… " I said lovingly. "I can't believe we have a son." I reached out cupping Xáne's face in my small hands, "Let's go get our baby back and give our daughter a funeral she never got."

The sadness crept on his face, "Yes, my princess deserves a funeral. She will be laid to rest but never forgotten."

I wrapped my arms around Xáne's neck and pulled him into me. That feeling of never seeing her again was something that was never going to go away, not for me or for Xáne, but we were going to do right by our princess and avenge her death. She didn't deserve this at all, and neither did her brother.

Chapter 10
Xánur

My entire body awakened when I felt Cin's plush body push up on me. Damn! I was trying my best to sleep, but not even that helped me. From the moment I kissed her and made love to her pussy, I couldn't see straight. Talking to Asar about what we were going to do or how we were going to find my son, couldn't stop images from conjuring up in my mind about how I could take her up the wall or fuck her for a week straight with recuperating time in the middle. I'd give her hours to herself, I'm not a monster.

Her ass rubbed against my dick one more time, and I groaned louder this time.

"Fuck, baby... Please, I'm trying here," Cin was definitely awake as she did it one more time. This time, she did it so slowly that I thought I was going to go nuts. My dick was so hard that I couldn't see straight.

I chuckled, this is how she wanted it... huh?

"Yes, that's how I want it, Xánur. Now, stop playing with me and give it to me as I like it," her voice was like its own aphrodisiac.

"You want it like the very first time?" I asked her as I manipulated the sheets to slide off her body making sure each part touched her most sensitive areas.

She moaned lowly, shaking her head.

"No, I want it like that time in your office. You remember that?"

I smirked as my fangs came out to play. I leaned in running the tips of my fangs over her bare shoulders. When did she get naked?

"If that's how you want it, my love, that's how you're going to get it."

My hand reached out gripping the back of her neck hard. I sat up, smiling wide as Cin turned laying on her stomach and spread her legs. I laughed as I gripped her waist with my free hand and lifted her up a bit. Instead of using a pillow, I pulled her closer to me making sure her thighs rested on mine for support.

"Oh, Xánur… " Cin's voice rose an octave as my thumb played with her clit. She wasn't able to move much in this position. I was going to give it to her as rough as she wanted it. "Stop playing with me, I want it, baby," my ego loved it and inhaled this like a drug. "Xán-."

I slid into her wet core cutting off her words. I didn't do it gently as I entered her with every inch.

"Fuuuuuuuuuu," Cin couldn't even finish her sentence as I pushed her head further into the pillows.

Her pussy seemed to gush some more at this action. Our bodies simply connected to each other, and I knew the atmosphere had changed. I lifted her body a little as I kneeled. She was at a very odd position not able to do a damn thing as I began moving.

"Give me what I deserved, Lucinda… " Her body seemed to shudder at how deep my voice became. She once described it as though it vibrated through every part of her body including her soul. "Fucking give it to me and don't you dare be selfish with this pussy, you hear me?"

My baby loved it when I talked to her like this. It drove her up the wall.

"Ohhh," she chuckled as she planted her palms on the bed and pushed up. She wanted a challenge.

"This is what you want to do, little girl? You want to show me who's boss?" I smirked letting go of her neck. Both of my hands were now gripping on her waist as she began to move.

I shut my eyes throwing my head back as I lost myself in everything Cin. Then, as if the world had tipped its axis, I became like a crazed animal. I felt it the moment my wings came out. I wanted this entire city, country, and world to hear who the fuck she belonged to.

I teleported us outside of the bedroom and landed on top of a cloud. Cin didn't have time to scream as I lifted her pulling all the way out to the tip, and then, slammed her back down on my dick. The friction of the cloud's softness tickled her nipples causing the tether to vibrate so hard in our bodies, I was sure the release of pheromones were released into the air. I heard as the Lycans, vampires, and every other creature smelled her arousal and what was going on. If they thought I was crazy before, then they would know tonight that I was meant to be committed a long time ago. I was fucking insane, and I loved it. Insanity had nothing on Cin's pussy and how it drove me past delirium.

I groaned like a wild animal. I leaned into her bypassing her shoulder as I sank my fangs into her neck. I could've been much gentler, but I felt the transformation the moment a drop of her blood hit my tongue, and I had to fight my talons from coming out so that they wouldn't sink into her waist. Cin's body froze for a moment, and she screamed out her orgasm as if I was punishing her for something. My dick refused to hit that high with her as I kept on moving through her creaminess. This was the best part, the sleekness, the sloppy, wet sounds that echoed through the night damning everyone in its vicinity because they would never be able to touch her or even get a taste of what was mine.

The way her walls gripped me made me want to split her apart just so I could get to her core then put her right back together to do it all over again. I ripped myself away from her neck as blood dripped from my fangs down to my chest and onto her back, but I could give a fuck about that. My right hand reached out, and as I ran my fingers down her back, they transformed into the talons digging lightly into her skin. I didn't draw blood, but Cin was on cloud nine at this point.

"Yes, Xáne, this! Fuck this is! Deeper, baby. Go so fucking deep!" She shouted.

I almost broke my resolve as I snickered. She wasn't as shy as she used to be, and I fell more in love. She thought she knew what I was going to do next, so I fucked it up for her when I pulled out of her, and I threw her in the air. Cin screamed as she fell down, then I teleported her back into the bedroom. When she landed on the bed on her back, I landed softly on top of her, threw her legs open, and slid in.

"Home," I grumbled as I moved my waist in a way I knew would cause her to cuss me out in three, two, one.

"You motherfucker! Ho-!" Her words ended in an endless moan as she came, and I was right behind her as I sunk deep into her as deep as I could get losing myself in her as I always did and would always do.

****

Lucinda

What the actual hell? That was all that I could come up with when I rubbed my ass on Xáne. Yes, sex with us was always great, but this was the first time I had ever been fucked in the literal air and thrown off as though he were going to kill me. Then, I was brought back for satisfaction. I wouldn't take any of it back, even though, I couldn't move the next morning.

I wish that I could say we only had sex once, but no, Xáne wasn't built that way. He didn't know what sleep nor rest was, and I, the lowkey nympho, had no problem saying yes. I could spread my legs open for Xáne and not care if he was rearranging my guts. That's how much I wanted it each time. My pussy cried out to me in the early morning when Xáne took me in the shower, but I told the little shit to shut her stupid ass whining up because I went three years without this man. If I could make it up in one night, I would, but I couldn't. Asar called out for Xáne in the morning, and he finally let me go to sleep.

I turned my neck towards the bathroom. It looked so far away, but I had to get ready for those damn sentinel lessons. I couldn't believe that I still had to do that but according to both Asar and Xáne, if we had a chance of even finding out who was responsible for what happened to me and finding our son, we had to keep doing whatever we were doing and for me to act as though some of my memories were gone. There was no way either Xáne or I was going to pretend like we weren't fucking each other again. Everyone would know not only by his scent on my body but also the way Xáne had a tendency to be up my ass wherever I was. I forgot how crazy this pussy made him.

****

When I entered into the training area, Asar stood with the other students just chatting it up as we had five more minutes before everything started. Asar had to be dramatic as he lifted his head up in the air and sniffed. He took a long sniff and turned his attention towards me with a smile on his face. I curled my upper lip and rolled my eyes as I threw my gym bag on the floor near the door with everyone else's. I had to get even more training in if I wanted to be ready for whatever fight was brewing in the air. I held my head high and straightened my shoulders as I masked the soreness trying to walk properly towards Asar.

The amusement was apparent on his face as I made it to Asar. "Really?"

He chuckled as he leaned in kissing my forehead.

"Finally, I can do that again without Xáne pummeling my head in."

I laughed lightly pushing him, "Now, you know damn well he's going to come in here stomping like a psycho and try to kick your ass again."

"Speak of the devil," Asar's eyes looked up, and I turned coming face to face with Xáne.

He leaned down, his face all up in mine.

"I do not stomp like a psycho, but I will fuck you like one right now if you want."

I narrowed my eyes at him, he wouldn't dare.

Asar laughed loudly behind me, "Leave her be, brother. She's walking funny already. She still needs to get through this session."

Xáne's face lit up as though Asar gave him a gift. He wiggled his eyebrows. I was confused by that but didn't have time to think as I felt his arm around my waist, and he pulled me into a mind-blowing kiss.

I melted into his arms forgetting how good of a kisser Xáne was. I moaned into his kiss, and Asar entered in both of our minds.

The youngins' are going to get a little too horny for this session if you don't stop. Yesterday was enough. I'm sure everyone wanted to fuck a wall at that point. Cut it out.

Xáne pulled away, and I stumbled for a moment. I eyed him up and down when I gathered myself again. *Who the fuck is this man?*

Xáne smiled as if I said something funny, "I'm your husband, woman and don't you forget it," he stated as he passed me. I felt his hand on my ass as he smacked it and gripped it hard.

My eyes widened. *This was definitely not my husband.*

"Yes, it is," Asar answered from behind me.

I turned facing him, "I thought you'd be out of my head, now."

Asar snickered, "Nope. Just out of your private conversations, but you weren't talking on that frequency now, were you, little girl?" He teased.

I gasped with my mouth open, "You heard that? How? His room is sealed."

"Oh, thank fuck for that. I heard it in his head. He can't stop replaying yesterday in that dirty ass mind of his."

I looked at Xáne as he was talking to the students and Jaya. He felt my eyes on him and glanced at me with a devilish grin on his face.

I'm going to kick your ass.

I spoke to Xáne privately as I conjured up a small fireball in my hand letting it wrap around my fingers.

Oh, bring it, baby. I'll fight you just like I fuck you, hard, rough, and at the end leave you sore.

Oh, I was definitely in love.

Chapter 11
Xánur

Cin's plush ass hit the mat for the umpteenth time, and I almost chuckled, but because she was so concentrated on beating me, I kept a straight face. She narrowed her eyes at me and gritted her teeth. She looked ready to set me on fire. The look in her eyes was all that I needed to confirm it, and just like that, the flames in her eyes lit up. It was the color of my eyes, and I couldn't help but feel my lips as they formed into a smile. I felt her fire within me. I exhaled missing this feeling. It must've been the years that we'd been apart, or else, I wouldn't be feeling like her flames were a part of me. As the flames seemed to lick within me, there was something she was seeing. Cin's flames were not burning me, but instead, they were caressing my soul. A part of me that no one but she had touched.

I watched her in admiration as she caught on to what was happening. Cin couldn't move from the position that she was in and neither could I.

What do you think it means Xáne?

She asked me.

I shrugged my shoulders not able to formulate a full sentence on what was going on. This was new even for me because now just as I could feel her flames in me, she could feel both the vampire and the rare werewolf in me. It's as if they were kindred.

It took us a while to snap out of it. It was like the time went on without us noticing as we just stood there trying to comprehend what had just transpired between us two. I knew what consisted of mating, but this was more than that, it was as if our souls had traded places. I saw myself in Cin much more than I could ever before.

****

The training session ended, yet I wasn't feeling like myself, so I didn't see it when someone rushed me the moment, we stepped out of the Sentinel building. I was picked up like I weighed nothing while Cin screamed my name as though I had died in her arms. I wasn't thinking as I began to move out of the hold trying to swing on the being who could remain incognito enough to run up on me. Then, when I heard his laughter, I stopped fighting.

"Really dad!" I shouted. "Put me down!"

If I didn't know this old bastard, then I would've never been ready for it when he let me go, and I dropped. I didn't even realize how high up we were until I looked down, he brought me so high up, you couldn't see the building anymore. I shut my eyes as I fell down with my arms wide open missing the air up here. It was weird. It's as if my father knew that I hadn't done this in so long and it brought a smile to my face as the wind blew through my hair at the speed that I was free falling.

When I got closer to seeing the building, my wings sprung out, and I flew over to where the building was. This had to be the best moment of my life besides seeing Cin again. I finally reached the ground with a thud that shook the ground. My eyes found what they were searching for, there my father was smiling proudly at me. The old man hadn't aged a bit, since I'd last seen him. I was the spitting image of him from the dark blonde hair to the pale blue eyes, except, his hair was longer than mine. His was down his back like Asar's and his father's as well. I was taller than my father by a few inches, but we were the same build.

The cheerfulness on his face was the opposite of what death represented, but I knew it was because he came to see me. Other than that, he'd be whispering the last words to souls, and none of them would be a gentle departing. I had as normal of a childhood as I could have for the era that I was born in. We were Vikings at the time, and my father adored me showering me with love so that I couldn't feel the loss of my mother. Majority of human women died during childbirth, especially, to beings like us. My father was not a Nephilim, he was a true, fallen angel, but others saw him as a god, the god of death. We never corrected them because more than half of what they said about him was true.

"My son," my father proudly said as I stood walking over to him. "You're a little slower than before. I might have to retrain you."

I scoffed, "Look here, you ancient being, if we ever fight, I'll drop your ass so quick that you wouldn't even know what happened." I couldn't help but join in when he started laughing. I missed that. Damn, how long has it been, since I've last seen him?

"Says the bastard that I snuck up on. Now son, I do forgive you," he stated as he turned to his left where a burning Cin stood. She was staring at me as though I had grown a third eye. My father kept talking, "I would be distracted, too if I had her walking with me. My dear, you are fascinating to look at."

I finally clued into what my father was saying as I stared at Cin. Were those wings? It was like the moment I noticed her fiery wings the crazy color that matched my eyes and hers. I blinked not sure what I was seeing, yet I don't think Cin had noticed. As I took a step towards her, my entire body felt like a heat rushed from my toes to my scalp. Cin stared at me with her mouth open as though she saw something I couldn't see.

I heard my Uncle Magni's voice, he sounded as though he was in awe.

"I told you, Xánur, that your son, you're last born, the only one to carry your own name, would change everything."

I turned. It was as if I didn't realize that my uncle had been standing there the whole time right next to Asar, whose hair was ruffled, which means my uncle caught him by surprise, too. I looked at my uncle who anyone could've mistaken him for being Asar's older brother, right along with my dad. Asar was an even more spitting image of his father than I was of mine. From head to toe, everything was the same, except, Asar had deep dimples that could be seen from miles away.

I faced Cin once more. She looked terrified much more than before.

"You're like me Xáne... " she stated.

I was confused by her words, until I focused on the reflection in her eyes. I was consumed by the flames, but I was not burning like before. No, somehow whatever Cin was, I became, and whatever I became, Cin was.

"They are finally complete," my father said, and I had never felt like such a child at this moment.

****

Lucinda

Staring into Xáne's eyes always made me feel like I would never worry about him falling out of love with me. Nothing he could ever do would make me feel that way, but the way he was gazing into my eyes as he transformed before into what I never knew existed, shook me to my core. I had never seen love personified in anyone's eyes, but in Xáne's that's where it morphed into more than just a feeling. This was a lifetime situation with us. I had never felt a soul, not even my own, but I knew it was there. I could feel Xáne inside of me from every cell, through my bloodstream, and I knew at this moment as we became the true meaning of kindred that we were never going to part. Someone would have to kill me to get me away from Xáne, and even then, my soul would always chase him because nothing in this world or the next, could rip it from us again.

He was beautiful. I had never seen anyone but myself that was engulfed by the flames, and they didn't burn, yet here my husband was matching me from head to toe.

"Your wings," Xáne said as he stood in front of me now.

I was confused, what was he referring to. What wings?

As I asked, it was as if I was seeing everything through Xáne's eyes. I saw how he saw me, and it was beautiful. The adoration in the way he watched me warmed me inside causing my flames to expand higher and higher. I reacted to what I saw from Xáne, and when I saw what he was talking about, I audibly gasped.

Wings! I had wings just as big as Xáne's flapping on their own in their glorious state. The way they moved, it was in unison with his. The pale blue of Xáne's eyes matched the flames. It was gorgeous, and I could feel as the tether between us became tighter. It was much more restraining, and it was as though the warning of the tether was spoken out loud to us.

Who you are is who I am... We aren't two separate entities because we were never separate to begin with.

We both took a step back not sure what the fuck that was! It was as though we unveiled another piece of the puzzle to whatever the hell was going on with us.

Just as I exhaled, a pain so fierce ripped through my body, and I threw my head back as I opened my mouth, screaming as though my heart was being ripped out of my body. I didn't realize at first what it was, but then, when my screams sounded deeper, rougher, and the scent of brimstone that I had never smelled before prompted me to open my eyes. I looked around trying to gauge what was happening, and then, there it was again. I saw myself through Xáne's eyes. The shock of what I saw caused me to stumble back knocking into whatever was in my path. I was too big to be out here. I had now become something that was impossible even for supes.

Before I could figure out how to formulate the words to say what it was, Xáne's father uttered them out loud causing everything in me to freeze.

"My God! How is this possible?" He exclaimed as though in awe. "She's a Dranix."

I clutched my chest, my eyes shutting from the sudden news. Right before I fainted, it occurred to me what it meant. I was the one supernatural that all of the supes were hunting for; a Dranix. A mix of a dragon and a phoenix.

Chapter 12
Xánur

I sat in my living room that felt way too small for us four now; Asar, the two old bastards, and I. Sitting back, I took a sip of my whiskey because I needed it, especially, right after what just happened. We wanted to talk while Cin was still passed out. I could feel how much that transformation took a toll on her. It drained her energy, and she needed to recharge.

"When were you going to tell me that she came back, son?" My father asked.

I turned to face him. I shrugged my shoulders, "Honestly, I don't know. I wasn't ever going to tell you because I thought I'd never forgive her for how she left me. Then, I found out the truth."

"What truth?" He asked.

"Someone made her leave. She didn't do it willingly, and in her mind, she was looking for her parents. Cin is an orphan. She never knew them, nor does she have any memory of them."

Both my father and uncle exchanged a look,

"What is it?" Asar asked. "What are you guys not telling us once again!" He shouted.

Father rolled his eyes. His eye twitched as though he was considering reaching out to smack the shit out of Asar for yelling. I snickered masking it as I chugged the rest of my whiskey. Father cleared his throat as he continued, "Had you two little shits not hid the fact that you and she were mated or rather married," he sent an accusatory glance both Asar and my way. "All your bastard ass had to do was let me meet her, and I could've told you everything about her. It's like you forget how fucking old I am or who I am."

"We could never forget how old you are," Asar joked, and father lifted his eyebrow as his eyes became black. Asar cleared his throat, "I'm messing with you Uncle X. Can't you take a joke? Jeez!"

"Boy… If I didn't have more information for you guys, I would've kicked your ass into the new millennium. Ungrateful, little punk."

Both Asar and I couldn't hold in our laughter. It felt good to see our family once more. The laughter died down quickly when we realized our fathers were close to really fighting us.

"Alright, we're serious… Go ahead, Father."

He scoffed, "Thanks," he said dryly. "I wouldn't have realized it nor believed her if I hadn't laid eyes on her. Do you know how long I've been searching for her son? She was my best fighting mate's daughter. Her name was Lissandra, the last of her kind, and someone, well rather the man who she fell in love with, used her. She was just as beautiful as your Lucinda is; from the straight black hair, the eyes, but the difference was that Lissandra was tall and almost as tall as us. She fell for someone who made her hide who she was. She shrunk in her size wanting to appeal to the human side of that monster, and in the end, he took advantage of her."

I was in shock. I had never thought to ask father if he knew of Cin's birth parents. He continued,

"Lissa was something else. You should've seen her fight, Son. We were all always in awe of her, but the moment that man, Victor, appeared into her life, we should've known. We were able to see everything else but that. By the time we found out what he did to her and how he took advantage of her, she was gone to us. Victor was what you would call a mad scientist even becoming much madder when your mother hid Lucinda from him. He wanted to experiment on her and see what would happen if he injected her with the virus."

I was trying to reign in my feelings of what I was learning about Lucinda's father, "How did she hide Lucinda from that fucking piece of shit?" I could feel the shifting happening, and if I wasn't careful, someone was going to die earlier than they should.

Uncle sighed, this time he spoke up, "Lissa had a best friend, Sirina, my ex." The surprise on my face made Uncle clear up what he was saying. "Others called her Hina and some Sirina, and she had a daughter named Hina with that bastard Victor. There was a reason why she sacrificed herself for both her best friend and her daughter, but I don't know why. We never found out why because we couldn't find Sirina's daughter or where Victor went. All we were left with were bodies of beings that we'd known since the beginning of our time."

I couldn't take any more information as I shut my eyes running my hands through my hair. I gripped my hair hard feeling like I should rip it from my scalp, but then, I had one more question, "Dad? You know how you can always find me no matter where I am in the world?"

"Yeah, what about it?"

I deeply inhaled and exhaled with eyes shut so tight that I felt a headache coming.

"I need you to teach me to find my son."

"Your son?" I heard the surprise in his voice.

I opened my eyes, staring into my father's eyes that were too much like mine, "Yes, I have a son, and he's out there somewhere. Where? I don't know, but as soon as I find him, whoever has hurt him will die by my bare hands, and I won't have to shift to do it. I want their blood on my hands, Father."

My father observed me for a moment, and then, a smirk appeared on his face, "Just as long as you give me their soul. I want to feast on it because no one touches a Helson and breathes to tell about it."

****

Lucinda

When I came to, I walked to the living room where I heard the men. Asar and Xáne's fathers were a surprise for me to see. I had never known that they would be so damn sexy. I didn't get a chance to really watch them, but now that I was standing there while they talked, they were as we would expect the product of two fallen angels to look like. They were full angels because of both of their parents. I had never thought any man in my life could be both gorgeous and rugged, yet here those two sat.

I wanted to announce my arrival, but the conversation took precedence over my presence. When I heard about what my father did to my mother and her best friend, my heart broke into pieces. It brought back memories to when I grew up in the supes orphanage hating my mother and father with everything in me, yet the only one that I should've given all of my hate for was him. That man was not my father nor was he human. How could he take advantage of a woman's love for him and force her best friend to have to endure such shit? My head was spinning with all of this information that was received. I stumbled as I heard Xáne making the declaration that was in my head the moment it came out of his mouth.

"Yes, I have a son, and he's out there somewhere. Where? I don't know but as soon as I find him, whoever has hurt will die by my bare hands, and I won't have to shift to do it. I want their blood on my hands, father."

I agreed with him without uttering it out loud. Today, I swore that the man who put his seed into my mother only to kill her and her best friend at the end, I would rip his heart out of his chest and make sure he saw who did it. Then, it felt like a ton of bricks hit me when a missing piece of my memory hit me hard. I couldn't call out any of their names, but I linked Xáne to my memory as I watched it unfold.

I went shopping downtown while Xáne and Asar were training. I had ditched practice because I wanted to look good for him. The feeling of something going wrong was buried deep in my guts, but I ignored it blaming it on being nervous. I was always nervous when it came to Xáne, even though, we'd been married for a couple of months now. I found a dress, paid for it, and made my way out of the store. Then, someone bumped into me so hard that I stumbled back. When I looked up, the man reminded me of a young Denzel Washington from his chocolate skin to the blinding smile. I tilted my head, there was something about him that I couldn't shake, "Do I know you?" I asked him.

He lightly chuckled causing all sorts of warning bells to go off in my head. He reached his hand out, and I took it standing as I waited for an answer.

"No, my little one, you don't know me, but you will."

There was a tone that he carried with him and I didn't like it. I pulled my hand out of his feeling like a part of me was drained.

Just as I opened my eyes to speak, he lifted his palm to his mouth and blew some weird contents on my face. I coughed trying to swat it away.

"What the fuck! Move!" I pushed him out of my way and began walking away, but it was like his voice carried with me, in my head slowly morphing into a woman's voice. One that I found peaceful and soothing.

Find your parents and leave Xáne, he can't help you... They are alive and looking for you as well.

I screamed so loud as if someone stole and ripped every part of me. I felt Xáne's arms around me as I dropped to the floor. He was here. He took everything from me.

Chapter 13
Xánur

Days. That's how long it took me to learn how to track my own damn son. The stress was eating away at my mind, and on top of that, feeling the anxiety that Cin was going through didn't help. In the back of my head, I knew I should've taken a day off, but I couldn't right now. There were too much, too many factors that were trying my patience, and if I didn't figure it all out, I was going to flip on someone.

I inhaled and exhaled as I heard Asar's footsteps behind me. I told him that I didn't want to stop for a moment, but he convinced father that I needed a break. Father was never pushy nor was he the type to tell you to quit unless you wanted to do it yourself. I removed the last piece of clothing I had on then I stood tall cracking my neck. It was Asar's idea not to go flying but instead to go running in the woods behind my place. I shut my eyes letting the transformation take place, this wasn't as painful as the first time it happened now it felt natural as I shifted. My paws hit the dirt, the sensations were different than when I was just a vampire. This was more as though I could hear not only the heartbeats of all who lived here but their blood, it called out to me. It smelled delicious, but it became intoxicating when both Asar and I began racing except my mind drifted towards the scents.

I didn't think, I couldn't think as I ran pushing down feeling the ground beneath me and the power that surged through my entire body freed my mind. In this moment, I wasn't thinking about anything, my mind was blank so blank that it became scary until I couldn't see what was in front of me because it was all a blur. I could still feel the dirt beneath me but now it was like my essence ran faster than me and entered a house. I had never been there before but everything about it looked familiar. Had I been here before? I stood there, shorter than I regularly felt but I was in a small blue bedroom. I eyed the bed, it was too small for me now, but I was afraid to tell her. Who was her? Then I surveyed the room, it was all in shambles, I didn't mean to shift but it suddenly happened overnight.

She was gone to work, and I promised her that I would be good. She didn't need to worry about me because I knew how to stay hidden yet somehow, I knew that this was going to cause her to spiral just like she did when my fangs grew. She was terrified because she claimed I was too young for it. I knew I was young but how old was I? Wait…

My essence froze as it realized that it wasn't me nor was it a memory. Something had just transpired. I pulled my essence from the body that it had just entered, and then, I was in shock as I finally came face to face with whose body I had just inhabited.

Who are you?

He asked me yet nothing could come to mind. He was speaking to my essence while he was in human form. Those eyes were my eyes and so was the dirty blonde hair. He kept it longer than I did when I was his age. He had his mother's nose. I knew he was mine from the moment my gaze fell upon him. Yes, he was young according to humans, but he was my son, a Helson so he was double his human age. While to humans, he was three, as a supe, he was six.

I'm your father.

He stood there watching me with eyes so damn pale blue and filled with such sadness, hopelessness and he was tired, my son was tired.

If you are my father, then you will come and get me. We've searched everywhere for you…

Just as I was about to ask him where he was, a voice called to him,

"Exra! I'm home!" The moment we lost eye contact, I was thrusted hard back into my body.

I came back into my own body not sure how we made it to the house, but I couldn't breathe as I shifted back. When I came to, it hurt me so fucking much to see my son and lose him again. I stayed on my knees not able to see anything at all. I knew I was having an anxiety attack, but I couldn't control anything.

"No!" I yelled out. "No! No! No!"

"Xánur!" I heard Asar calling my name out, alarmed yet none of that could snap me back.

I cried out, hard as if someone had taken my very soul from me. I tried to stay strong when I first saw our daughter's limp body in Cin's arms in her vision but this... No! not this. When I was ripped away from my son, I saw the image of my daughter as she protected my son in the womb. She knew that something was wrong, and she repositioned herself in front of him shielding him from whatever was going to come to pass.

I yelled louder, rougher until my voice was hoarse. I felt the tears as they fell from my eyes and nothing, no one could make me stray away from avenging my deceased daughter. She didn't deserve this. None of us deserved this. Whoever separated us didn't need to be afraid of my father's wrath because I would make sure that it rained blood and sulfur on this very earth because no one touched my family. NO ONE!

****

Lucinda

I watched over Xáne as he was out on the bed. He slept on his stomach with his hair all over the place, he was finally at peace. Well, not really but putting him in the induced sleep was his father's doing. Xáne was having an anxiety attack to rival all anxiety attacks. He had set fire to the woods with just his emotions and when I got out there, he didn't even recognize me through the fog that took over his mind. He kept crying out calling our daughter and our son, he saw something, but we couldn't calm him down long enough to tell us.

I reached out running my hand through his hair. I smiled when he did. He knew who I was even in his sleep, yet in that moment not too long ago, he didn't know me. He didn't see any of us, and it worried me. He worried me. I gazed at the tattoos on his back that he had elaborated on over the past couple of days; A big angel with his wings open in the middle of his back, a prayer inside the clouds from his shoulder blades and covering his neck, and on his lower back was a sad baby angel. I didn't ask him what it meant, but I knew it had something to do with what has happened to us. I watched him as he breathed in and out. I loved this man too much to let him lose it before we ended our enemies. I found out a long time ago that I wasn't the type of female that would sit back and let her enemies continue on living. Nope, I was the type to let them know that their time was running out and as soon as I spotted them, everything that they knew and loved would disintegrate within my reach. Why? Because they touched my husband and my kids. No one caused my husband this much pain and lived to see tomorrow.

I sighed knowing that he wasn't going to be getting up right now but as soon as I stood, he groaned.

"Stay," his voice was so damn hoarse. It didn't even sound like him anymore.

I slid into bed with him getting under the duvet. His arm wrapped around my waist as he pulled me into him. I shook my head this man was still able to know his surroundings even though the sleep that he was in was supposed to be deeper than the average one. I mean, his father was death, for all we know. If he was human, he would be dead right now.

****

Xáne didn't wake up a couple of hours later, yet he didn't let go of me. He held on tight as though if he let me go, he'd never wake up again. I heard heavy footsteps entering the room. I glanced towards the door, and it was Xáne's father. He looked like he hadn't slept in years.

"He still won't let you go?"

I shook my head, "Nope. Guess, this whole forever term is even when he's in this state. Do you know what put him in that condition?"

"Come," His father stretched his hand out to me when he got closer. "Let's talk in the other room."

As I made the attempt to get up, Xáne growled and pulled me closer to him almost crushing me.

"Mine," he growled. I faced him, yet he was still asleep. Why the hell was he so strong?

I rolled my eyes, "I guess we're going to have to talk in here then?"

Xáne's father chuckled, "We'll wait until he's up. I know when I'm not wanted somewhere. He may be in deep sleep, but I know my son well, and right now, he only wants you with him. Entitled, little bastard."

I lightly laughed. "Did you raise him alone?" I asked him before he walked out.

Xáne's father gazed at his son adoringly nodding his head.

"Yeah, I did. Raising a son without a mother is difficult. As you can see, his mother was nowhere to be found, but it wasn't because she didn't want to be. It's that she couldn't. When I had him, my last born, all his siblings had died. Having a child with a human at that time was extremely detrimental to both the lives of the babies and the mother. Xáne was the only one to survive. His mother didn't. I made sure to love him for the both of us because that woman, I loved the fuck out of her, but she is no more, of course, and now, this old bastard just sucks souls out of people's bodies," he shrugged his shoulders as if it was nothing.

This was something I didn't know about Xáne and it saddened me. "I'm so sorry," I didn't know what else to say.

He smiled at me, "Oh, dear girl, don't stress yourself with feeling sorry for me. Had Xáne not met you first, I would've ravished you and had you addicted to me before you could learn of my true nature." He winked at me as he walked out.

I knew I looked stupid as ever as Xáne's father walked out of the room while my eyes were probably as wide as saucers, and my jaw was wide open out of shock. Holy hell! If I didn't know before, I know now. Xáne got all his charm from his father; the sexy, dangerous, daring, and dark charm of his.

As I laid back on the bed, Xáne's words flowed from his mind over to mine.

No one could ever beat a Helson, not even in revenge.

I shivered as a cold chill ran through my body. I smiled wickedly at nothing as I answered him.

No baby, no one can.

Chapter 14
Xánur

I was in a deep sleep state, and I knew it, yet I couldn't wake up until my father's touch wore off on me. I wanted to tell Cin that our child was so beautiful, tall, and he looked like the spitting image of me. I couldn't get the awe of being a father and seeing my son for the first time out of my head. My essence traveled beyond my body leaving my surrounds. Even though my arm was still around Cin, everything else soared making its way back to the same room, my son's room.

This time, Exra was ready for me. It was as though he felt me coming. He was sitting down on the floor as he had a sketchpad and a pencil. I watched him for a moment admiring the fact that I had an offspring of my own. Before meeting Cin, I had never thought about children, but now, I couldn't see us without kids.

"You made it," he said to me as he gazed up at me.

Again, the fact that I had a son shook me to my core. I kneeled not wanting to tower over him. I couldn't help the smile that appeared on my face. He was the reason for this joy, and he felt it too.

"You knew I'd come?" I asked, curious to see how strong he was.

"Yes, I did. The link that I've always felt became stronger from the moment you first stepped into my room. You're much more than I expected," he admitted.

"Me too, Exra. Me too. You speak so eloquently, and you look so much older than your age. I've missed so much." I was going to spiral if I didn't get a hold of myself. I shut my eyes needing a moment.

Just then, as if he knew what was going to happen. I felt his touch. Exra hugged me, and it broke my world into pieces. I didn't know what I did to deserve this, but I wrapped my arms around him hugging him.

"Thank you. Thank you for being alive and not hating me or your mom. We didn't know. I'm so sorry."

"My mom? She's alive?" He didn't leave my arms. Instead, he laid his head on my shoulder.

This didn't feel like a first meeting. If anything, it felt like we've been in each other's lives for so long. I nodded, "She is, and she's desperate to meet you. That's why I'm here. I need to know where you are."

He moved out of the hug, and he stared at me for a moment.

"If I tell you where I am… will you take Hina away from me? I have to protect her. She doesn't know, but he's found us, and we have to leave this place soon."

My breath hitched, "Who is he and where is this place?"

"He is my grandfather, and Auntie Hina said that this orphanage would keep us safe. She said my mother, if she was alive, she'd know where this was. He knows that I'm alive now, and he's going to kill her for hiding me."

"She hid you?" My mind was going a mile a minute. "Okay, okay… how do you know where he is?"

I knew I was asking a lot from my kid, but he was stronger than I was when I was a kid. I could feel it.

"She did, and I know because I can feel him no matter where I am. I am a part of him. Not like you and my mother but because he is still blood I can feel him when he is getting closer. He's on this side of the world. The supes side."

The news shocked me, and before I could find out more… I was pulled out of his room.

****

I could've murdered whoever pulled me out, but when I realized it was my father, I calmed down, or so I thought, until I was out of my bed and yelling at my father like I had lost my mind.

"Are you fucking kidding me? I was talking to my son. Why would you pull me out like that?"

Father cocked his eyebrow, "Come again?"

"Are you deaf, old man? I said I was talking to my son, and you had no right pulling me out like that. Had you just entered my mind, you would've seen it!" My father swung and had I been paying attention, I would've ducked, but it was too late.

My jaw cracked. He broke my fucking jaw, and I saw red. I growled not even taking it in that I shifted morphing into a cross between the vampire and the wolf. My father hadn't had the chance to see me shift into a werewolf. I didn't think as I attacked him. He was fast but not fast enough due to the extra boost I had from being both. I heard Asar and Uncle Magni yelling for me to stop, but nothing could stop me from attacking. Father's eyes shifted, and he transformed into what others called the grim reaper, but he was more than that. He was scarier than that too, yet I didn't relent. He didn't look like I did. He was all black from head to toe. There wasn't any part of him that you could see as a different supe. He was just black, and the moment that roar came out of his mouth, lava spilled from his mouth landing on my floor causing it to melt.

"You want to fight me, you ungrateful fucking shit. You think you can take me because of who you are now? I'm your father. I will always one-up you. Magni hold him down. He doesn't notice what the fuck he just did."

I didn't give a damn nor flinch at his threats. I heard Uncle's thunder as it crackled in the air. When I was younger, that used to scare me shitless but not anymore. Right now, it made me mad that he wanted to step in. Had I not been so mad, I would've understood, but I was way past that point. I was hit by something in my rib. I flinched, but it didn't knock me down. I knew that feeling from anywhere. It was my Uncle's hammer passed down from his father, the Norse god, Thor.

"If you want to end me now, father, do it yourself and stop letting others do your dirty work. However, think about it, had it been me that was missing, and you found me, what would you do? Would you fight your father like you did the first time he wanted to kill me too? Loki was his name, wasn't it? And you think that it's okay, right? That you could protect me from him, yet you can't let me protect my own son? He NEEDS me!"

I saw the hesitance in my father's eyes, even though, they were all black. I knew every movement he made even when he completely disappeared and appeared in front of me.

"If you want to save your son, then I suggest you calm your ass down, right the fuck now, Xánur, and I mean it."

He raised his hand placing it on my shoulder. I flinched hard as the lava burned through the flesh. It was worse that my flesh was healing at the same time that it was burning. I took a breath in and breathed out through the pain that he knew he was causing, "Cin knows where our son is." I concentrated on the room searching for Cin who was in the corner not wanting any part of this. She looked on the verge of tears at my declaration. "He said it's the only orphanage that would protect them, and you know where it is."

Cin gasped, "It's the orphanage I grew up in. It has to be. Xáne..." I told her never to cry. I can't handle it when she does.

I didn't even realize I shifted, and the room smelled like burned skin as my father let me go. I stopped in front of her, cupping her face in my hands.

"Let's go get our baby boy and kill all those who've caused you to cry. I think it's about that time, don't you think so?"

She nodded, agreeing with me.

****

Lucinda

I was jittery and couldn't calm my nerves as we drove out to the orphanage. It was weird. I didn't remember the last time I'd gone there, but I had this deep feeling inside of me that made me want to go there. However, I kept putting it off ever since I came back to this side. This was it! Xáne and my son, Exra, were the pull that made me come back. I had to meet them two again and reunite with them. When I was making my way back to this side of the world, the pull was so strong that I felt it wrapping its imaginary collar around my throat and pulling me hard.

Xáne's hand covered mine as we stopped in front of the orphanage. That same pull was so strong that I couldn't properly breathe. His hand squeezed mine hard, and I knew Xáne was just as nervous as I was. Our son was literally twenty minutes away from us, and we both didn't know this. How is it that we lived in the same city as him, yet we never encountered each other? There were so many questions swimming through my mind right now, and I couldn't shut them out until I turned. The moment I did that, my eyes landed on the most precious little boy who I knew was mine. I choked on my own breath as those pale eyes gazed into mine. He knew who I was, and I knew who he was.

I shook harder. I wasn't a crier but ever since I've been back, all I did was cry, and at this moment, these tears were worth it. The son that I carried in my womb was standing a couple of steps away from me. He was alive, and he survived. My door opened. I knew it was Asar who opened it, yet I couldn't look away from my son. He was bigger and taller than I expected it. He was beautiful, and I was so in love. This was the first time I met him, yet it didn't change anything nor did I waiver in my steps toward him. The blonde hair that was up in a ponytail showcased his father's features, and then, as I got closer, my features appeared. He had my nose.

I stopped in front of him just staring down at what was mine, and he looked up at me. I was too scared not sure on what I should be doing in this moment, but before I could make a decision, Exra's little arms came around my waist, and he hugged me. I broke down as I hugged him back. I was terrified that he would hate me for not being there for him, for not searching for him until now, but this was my child. He forgave me just as I forgave my mother when I found out it wasn't her fault.

The instant I felt Xáne's arms come around covering mine over Exra, I felt my entire body come alive. This moment, this tether between us three was never going to break. Each tether was different; the one I had with Xáne was because we were bound to each other forever, and the one each of us shared with our son was on its own magnitude. I knew Exra felt it too.

"I knew you would find me, Father," Exra said, and I knew he was crying too.

This was a chance we all needed even before we realized we wanted it. I would never trade this for anything else.

"I will always find you, Exra," Xáne said.

****

The reunion didn't last too long in front of the orphanage as we took both Hina and Exra out of there before anyone knew we were there. Now, here we were all staring at each other as Exra sat next to Hina as though he was her protector. I didn't feel bad or anything because he reminded me so much of Xáne as he watched all of us. He was on alert, even though, we were his parents, he needed to be sure that we were not his enemy. I saw the look in his eyes as he took in all the giants in the room.

I turned facing Asar who hadn't stopped staring at Hina. I spoke to him telepathically.

Stop staring at her dude! You're being a fucking creep!

He didn't even care as he continued to do it.

She's so damn beautiful, I can't look away. Now, I know how Xáne felt the moment he saw you. I can't control my eyes, no matter how hard I try to turn away, they come back to her. Fuck, she's gorgeous.

I almost rolled my eyes but stopped the action as Xáne interrupted us as he spoke to Asar.

Well, keep your dick in your pants. She's like family technically.

Asar laughed not caring how everyone eyed him suspiciously.

I've never been happier to say that; you and I are not related by blood. I could kiss our grandparents Thor and Loki for never being related...It was all for this moment because, she is mine. I can feel it in my bones and yes, my dick is included.

Before either of us could reply, Asar stood making his way to where Hina sat on the couch. He stretched his hand out, and she reciprocated. He smiled like a territorial maniac and his mouth opened, "Let me introduce myself. I am Asar Ragna, your mate, your husband, and the only man that you will love for the rest of your life."

My eyes widened at this declaration.

What the hell just happened?

Chapter 15
Xánur

In less than six months, my life had transformed from being an angry individual who carried his hurt everywhere and lashed out at whoever I could. It felt weird but right, especially, at this moment as I walked into Vali's welcoming party for both my queen and my father. The moment the big, double doors opened to the grand hall, all those who were speaking had stopped as they gawked at my entire family coming in as a unit. Today wasn't going to be just a party. No, it was going to be a blood bath. I could've waited to analyze the situation at hand, but when it came to my gut feeling, I followed it.

I know most of the supes and royals in attendance were in awe of my father and my uncle. They were legends that never bothered to show their faces unless a war broke out, yet here they were… a war was brewing. Vali's face was priceless as he sat on his throne in an all-black suit with the crown on his head. I tilted my head watching him as he just sat there with a smug expression on his face, but the moment I bared my fangs, it disappeared off his face. I shouldn't have laughed the moment my eyes landed on Jaya as she sat in the queen's chair, yet that was the first thing that came out of my mouth. She stared wide eyed at me as though she thought I was going to have her a different reaction, but I smiled wickedly at her.

Her eyes moved from mine to Cin as she had her hand in mine and to my son as he stood on the opposite side of me. She took everyone in from Asar who stood behind me with Hina by his side and then last but not least, my father and uncle. Her breath hitched and her heartbeat sped up when she looked back at Hina, there was recognition in her eyes. I didn't turn around to see Hina's reaction, but I felt the sharp intake from her, and I knew something was off. I lightly chuckled, I knew Jaya had something to do with this. There was always a feeling that she never wanted me just because and that she was right in front of me all the time that she became familiar.

"I guess Jaya chose a side," Cin said to me as we stood in the center of the room.

I looked down at Cin smiling as though it was my birthday. She was fucking beautiful, and I couldn't believe that she was here with me today. I was and will always be the luckiest man, vamp, and creature alive. She was stunning. I couldn't take my eyes off her when I set them there.

"My queen, please go take your rightful place," my own voice deepened as she smirked.

"Thank you, my King. I'll go prepare the throne for you to sit on."

My eyes followed Cin as she strutted toward the throne seats. Her rose gold dress shimmered down the black carpeted aisle. Cin stopped walking turning to face, and I took her in as she winked at me. I'd fuck her right here if we didn't need to do this first. Her smile awakened every part of me that I was trying my best to suppress. Her dress licked every part of her; my eyes traveled from the deep V-Neck, then it held tight around her waist, and she had those double splits she loved so much. The fact that it was long sleeved was hilarious to me because Cin was always full of surprises. She turned back around, and her hair in its natural glory of coils made me want to run my fingers through it. I hadn't seen it in that state in so long. She always wore it straight.

Cin turned back around with an outstretched arm. The flame started from her elbow as it traveled to her palm and licked her fingers, too. When she finally got in front of Vali and Jaya, she began to speak. She turned first to Jaya, "Didn't you always want this position, dear Jaya? You know I wondered what it was that caused me to keep going further and further away, although, I had so much more in store for me here with my husband," Cin turned back to look at me and gave me a pouty expression, "Baby… did you know that she was the woman's voice that I could never place?"

I was shocked by this statement and wasn't even sure what to say. This took even me by surprise. She took my girl away from me and decided to ride my dick like that shit was all good? I shook my head ready to step in, but my father's hand landed on my shoulder. I turned to look at him, and he had that wicked smile I sported not too long ago.

"Let your queen show these people why she is a Helson, my son. She is much more than any of them will ever be."

I nodded and turned back to watch what she was going to do next. Cin sighed as she cracked her neck, and Jaya was being pulled out of her seat. I wanted to clap at my powers that Cin absorbed.

"Kneel," Cin barked the command at Jaya. She was a small little thing but as she stood there in all of who she was, I was in awe.

Jaya's eyes showed such anger towards Cin, and she even took a daring step closer, but Cin laughed like it was amusing to her. She threw her head back as she shifted. This was the second time I saw her shift and still, my heart beat for her in a crazy way. She wasn't a full dragon. No, she was better; Wings that were twice her size made of flames, the essence of the dragon hovering over body showing who she was and then the icing on the cake, the crown made of flames on her head showcasing that she was in fact the true queen.

The growling came from her and the scent of brimstone mixed with cinnamon filled my nose. I inhaled deeply, so deeply that I instantly became high off it.

"Kneel." She said once more to Jaya.

Now, Jaya, she was a warrior through and through, yet at this moment, she was terrified. She gritted her teeth as she kneeled before Cin. This was amusing to Cin as she laughed harder causing the whole place to shake.

She faced Vali who stood without being told as he kept a watchful eye on both my father and my uncle. He knew what went down when these two were involved, but then, every second his eyes kept going towards Hina. He watched her intently as though he were in love with her, but she never looked his way. I cocked my eyebrow when his eyes landed on mine. He didn't say anything as he removed the crown from his head making his way towards me. When Vali stood in front of me, I bowed my head ready to get the crown on my head, but Exra screamed out.

"No!"

Before I could know what was going on, Exra, my son, shifted before my eyes. I had never seen anything like it. His essence was triple his size showing more of a dragon as his flames burned pale blue, orange, and violet. His eyes were not all black like mine. Instead, they matched the violet of the flames. He had the talons though, and his fangs came out. We all just stared at him as he threw the crown on the floor roaring loudly at Vali.

All hell was about to break loose.

****

Lucinda

My son, our son was something that I had never had the chance of setting my eyes on, and it made me proud when he shifted. I never knew he could do that, yet he had. He was the most terrifying being in there besides his grandfather, his uncle, his great uncle and none other than his father. I shifted back to my human self as I went towards the queen's seat that Jaya thought was hers and sat in making sure to place one leg over the other. The entire seat was set ablaze by me sitting in it, and I felt like I was home.

I watched as my son reached for Vali's neck quicker than anyone else, and I was in shock. He growled like everything else in the world was going to die in his hands. Just as he squeezed, there was this feeling, a tugging as I had felt it the very first time. I turned towards the left, and there a man, the same man that I once saw who blew some weird substance in my face watched me as I watched him. Nothing else mattered as time slowed down for me, I deeply breathed in and out, not able to control myself. The moment I stood to go toward him and kill him, Jaya's fist connected with my face. In this instance, I saw red as I attacked Jaya with all my might.

I needed to get closer to this man and end his life for taking my daughter from me, but Jaya wanted a fight, one that she thought she would win. I didn't even know where I began or where she ended. She must've thought that being tall as hell gave her the advantage, but she forgot that I learned from the best, my husband. I wanted to fight her with just my strength, but I had to kill that man. He took everything from me; my mother, my daughter, and my sister. I never got to grow up with Hina. She was quiet, timid, and she didn't speak unless she had to. This angered me; the fear in her eyes as any and every man approached her. I felt every bit of her strength, yet she didn't display it. My vision cleared for a moment as I found myself on top of Jaya, my small fists raining blow after blow. I was so angry that I had a sister out there that I never looked for. She suffered while I lived protected on the other side of the world. My daughter, oh my poor daughter lost her life, all for what? He was a nobody, and he had people like this helping him.

I unleashed the cry that I was holding in as I shifted. I didn't think about my actions as I wrapped my hands around Jaya's throat not holding back and increased my flames. I heard her cries as I submerged her in my fire, and I didn't care because all that she did wasn't worth saving her life. I didn't stop until I heard a strained cry from far away in the room, that was the only sound that caused me to stop. I looked in the corner where my so-called father was a moment ago, and I saw a little girl who was a human flame like me crying as she stared at me. I stumbled back as I recognized that flame color. It was the violet that was in Exra's eyes and flames. This was his twin, and I couldn't breathe. There was no way... my daughter was dead and before I could think, my body led me toward her.

I couldn't stop until I kneeled in front of her. Was she real or was this part of my imagination? I inhaled and exhaled.

"Please..." I cried, "Please, let this be real." I whispered not sure who I was talking to.

"You can see me?" The little girl's sweet voice filled my ears and I just stared.

"Yes," I cried again. "I can see you. Can you see me?" She nodded.

As she was about to say something, it occurred to me that everything had gone to hell. The noise flooded in now, and it was mayhem in the ballroom. As I was about to turn, my son appeared in front of me and his sister. They didn't say anything but as they stared at each other, they merged into one being. I'd say that it was the creepiest yet most fascinating thing alive. I dropped from my knees to my ass. What the hell had Xáne and I birthed? I didn't get a chance to ask as they disappeared from in front of me.

I turned to see where they had gone, and I scrambled to my feet to get to Xáne. Something was wrong with him as he was on his knees kneeling in front of my father as though he had admitted defeat. He couldn't see as my father raised his hand with a sword in his hand but before he could strike, my children appeared behind him and stuck their right hand in his back pulling it back as they ripped his heart out of his chest. It was as if reality set in, and I ran toward all of them.

"Xánur!" I yelled out his name as I finally made it to him just realizing now that I must've looked insane.

I lifted his head, yet there was this fog in his eyes.

"Fuck! Xáne! Shit..." I cupped his face in my hands, yet it was as if he couldn't see me.

Then, Xáne began to cry as though he was seeing a different reality.

"Cin... my poor love, Lucinda, how could you just off and die on me? How could you leave me like this HUH!" He screamed out with so much anger, he caused all the lights to shut off in the ballroom and all that was left was our children's flames.

I slapped Xáne yet nothing. It wasn't working and even the fighting around us stopped. I heard as his father, his uncle, Asar and Hina ran to us, but there was nothing I needed from them. I needed Xáne. I didn't care that I never got to ask my father about why he did it nor did I care about Jaya's crisped body or why Vali was ripped in half... All I cared about was this man right in front of me. The man that I would move the entire earth for and without him, I would die. Nothing would ever make sense again if he didn't love me as hard as he did.

Tears spilled out of my eyes as I inhaled and exhaled. There was only one thing I had to do, and I knew I risked killing him just as much as killing me. I didn't ask for anything of anybody but Asar.

You fucking watch my kids... do you hear me you bastard? You love them just as hard as Xáne and I would love them.

He was confused.

What does that even mean?

He asked but I ignored his inquiry as I hugged a distraught Xáne and set us both on fire. I concentrated on the fire deep within me. The flame that was conjured from our tether, the bond that we always had, the one that would never let us separate no matter what or where we were. The bond that had both of our abilities acting a fool when we first met. I needed that tether that comforted us when no one wanted us to be together. The one that was screaming to us now, to fight, to keep going and to never give up.

I thought of our wedding day, the one that where he showed me just how much he loved and treasured me. It was in this grand-hall that I took those steps towards him with Asar giving me away. When I was walking down that aisle, I swore to myself that I would love this man till death and even in death, I would love him even harder because both life and death were eternal for us. When he removed the veil from my face, the way he looked at me spoke on so many levels. His love shined through his eyes, the words he spoke to me and the ones I gave him were us. Nothing and no one could take that from us.

"Though the fire may seem like it is burning you, it will never consume you…" I said to him with a smile on my face.

And his words… I would never forget. He had a smirk on his face as though he knew I would never stop loving him.

"Death will come for you, take over your everything, and even consume you, but one thing death won't do is ever put out your fire because baby, your fire burns for me and only me."

Chapter 16
Xánur

To say that I expected all of this would be to lie, but I should've known that all our enemies would be closer than we thought. I blacked out when I saw Jaya's fist connect with Cin's face. She was always my first priority and would always be my weakness. If she was hurt, then I was hurt, and no one could tell me differently. I should've paid much more attention to my surroundings and that Vali's men were in disguise. One alarming thing was when Vali came over to give me the crown, he had a look in his eyes that I could not decipher. It was not like him at all, and it threw me off but when my son intercepted the placing of the crown on my head, I knew it.

Whatever was on the crown spread like wildfire because everything broke out into a fight. Every royal there that had been there since I could last remember began fighting. We were having our very own war in that ballroom, and none of us cared about who was going to stay alive or not. All we thought about was killing. I moved my son's arm from Vali as I charged Vali blindly not caring about what was being said or going on. We should've checked what the hell was on that crown and it should've been questioned as to how long it had been on there but the air… the scent in the air that spread like wildfire was war and we as Nephilims, fallen angels, hybrids, and all other supes ingested that proving to ourselves how deadly we could become.

I shifted throwing Vali off. As he took a couple steps back, I launched at him not thinking twice as I reached for his lower abdomen with my teeth. I hadn't killed anyone as the were-vamp mix that I was. The blood thirst that flowed through my body made my entire body shudder as I ripped through him as though he were a rag, but then, something made me let go. I took a step back and eyed Vali; his body was torn, shredded even in half, yet he was still breathing. Even with his guts literally spilling, the look in his eyes bothered me. I knew that expression.

It was of a broken-hearted man and a hopeless man at that. What was I missing?

There I was, with blood spilling out of my mouth and Vali staring at me as though he were trying to tell me something. I didn't want to, but I took that moment to enter his mind and I had never seen anything like it. There was nothing there but darkness surrounding it. At a far, far corner there was a huge golden cage with a naked man staring at me, yet he looked like he wasn't all there. He just stood there and as I got closer and closer in his subconscious, the man became visible in the face... It was Vali himself. I was in shock as I stood there watching him as he watched me, the caged man gripped the bars of the cage shaking it like a madman.

"Get me out of here!" He shouted, "I need to get out! My girl, my mate, she needs me! I have to go to her!"

"Your mate?" I shouldn't have been in his mind this long, but it was as though I had to stay and find something out.

His eyes landed on mine, bugged-eyed he answered me, "Yes, Sirina... Where is she? I searched for her. I truly did and then I was stuck in here. Someone took over my body!"

I took a step back, the revelation of it all wretched me out of his mind as he screamed like a madman again.

"Don't leave me here! Save her!"

****

When I came too, Victor stood in front of me, and now, I saw where Cin got her eyes from but before I could attack, he blew some weird substance in my eyes. I yelped first as though someone took over my mind and then I opened my mouth to scream out, but nothing came out. The substance took over my vocal chords, the feeling was excruciating. The only thing that had burned me this way was Cin's flames, but that never drove my body into a spasm. I shifted back to my vampire self then as I took the scene in, the chaos had turned bloody. There was blood everywhere, was I the only one left alive? I looked around. I saw my father, death himself just staring back at me yet his eyes were lifeless. It didn't make any sense because that was impossible, no one could kill death, or could they? I whimpered as I took a step towards him but then I tripped over another body, it was my uncle's and he was just as gone as my father.

I shut my eyes, crawling on my knees as I searched for Cin, my son as well but I couldn't see them at first. I saw Asar as he laid his body over Hina's, he died protecting her yet they both didn't survive. At this, my tears began to escape blurring my vision and then I heard him speak,

"at last, we meet," I turned to face the voice and I saw Victor. He was smiling and I stood teleporting in front of him. I growled but he didn't even flinch. "You failed her. Just like Magni and Vali both failed Sirina. Isn't it funny that two powerful men were in love with Sirina yet couldn't save her from me? Me, a mere human being?"

Victor threw his head back laughing as if this was the funniest thing ever. I wiped my tears from my eyes.

"Give me her body right now." I tried to shift but nothing worked.

"Bow to me first, and then, I will give her to you. You'd do anything for her wouldn't you? Won't you give her a proper burial? One you never gave your daughter?"

Each word was like a nail to my heart. Everything I have ever lived for was for her and my family. Nothing mattered to me if I couldn't have her or my son and as for my daughter, I was so sorry to her that I didn't hesitate as I got on my knees. The thud that they made to that floor was the loudest thing I had ever heard.

Cin's body appeared before mine with a knife to her heart and her eyes... oh those beautiful eyes that I adored and loved to look at. I needed her to look at me just one time. To smile at me and tell me how much she loves me. She was my joy, my strength, my everything. I couldn't hold it in as I cried. In this moment, I could've laughed at myself for saying I had become someone who doesn't stop crying but this wasn't funny at all or was it a dream... I was all alone, and I lost all the people who mattered to me. I was surrounded and drenched in the blood of everyone I knew and loved. I reached out caressing Cin's cold cheek turning her head towards me,

"Cin… my poor love, Lucinda, how could you just off and die on me? How could you leave me like this HUH!" I shouldn't have shouted at her but what was it that she promised me? That she would never leave even in death but she's dead, yet her spirit is gone from me.

"Any last words?" Victor taunted me.

I could've gotten up and killed him but what would that have done for me? Instead I laid Cin's body down to the ground and stood. I grabbed his head and bit him without thinking, this time releasing venom instead of sucking his blood. I let him go and he stumbled back grabbing his neck as though he didn't expect that from me.

"The venom of death will always accompany you wherever you go and when you finally die, you will be sent to my favorite chamber in my father's house… the room of death."

I kneeled back to Cin's body as I said my vows to her once more hoping that she knew that I would forever love her even if she was gone from me.

"Death will come for you, take over your everything and even consume you but one thing death won't do is ever put out your fire because baby, your fire burns for me and only me."

As I finished saying those words, I felt her flames erupting from inside of me and as I threw my head back fire released from my mouth. The fire engulfed every part of me and her wrapping itself around us as though it were a cocoon yet this time nothing burned but my mind then everything became pitch black… Was this a dream or had I just felt Cin's lips on me as though she were happy to see me?

****

Lucinda

I was exhausted. This was all too much for me and trying to break whatever my father did to Xáne drained me much more than I thought it would. When I came to, we were back in our room. I didn't have any idea how we got back but I figured we were brought back. I looked around, searching for Xáne to make sure he was okay, but he wasn't in the room. Without thinking about much or just letting the moment sink in to feel my tether, I leaped off the bed almost busting my ass as I made my way out of the room.

I ran through the hallway, running down the stairs not even taking in who was around. I ran passed the living room straight to the kitchen but that voice that I was searching for,

"Why is your heart beating like that?" I never wanted to cry more than now hearing his voice.

I turned to face him as he stood behind me.

"Xánur…" I didn't even think twice as I jumped on him and he pulled me up.

I wrapped my arms around his neck, my legs around his waist as though I would never let go of him again. I didn't even think twice as I moved my head back a bit kissing his entire face as I ran my fingers through his hair. Tears fell but I didn't care because Xáne was okay, I was okay… we were okay. Just then I heard laughter causing me to stop what I was doing. I looked to my right and my heart felt like it grew three times more; my daughter stood there giggling at what I was doing to her father. She was real. I gasped as I looked at her, she was so beautiful. The first thing I noticed were her hazel-gray eyes, they were mine through and through. Her hair was dark like mine but everything else was her father. The resemblance was uncanny; from the way her face lit up when she giggled to the facial features.

"She's beautiful," I whispered.

Xáne held me closer as he also whispered, "Isn't she? Her name is Phoenix," Xáne informed me.

I let go of Xáne, as he put me down, I couldn't stop staring at her. I thought she was gone from us yet here she was. My palm went to my chest, I didn't know what else to do as I stood there. I felt Xáne's palm on the small of my back lightly pushing me towards her, "Go on… Don't be shy, say hi."

Had this was something else, I'd roll my eyes at Xáne but that light shove was needed. I walked on trembling legs as I got closer to her. Her eyes lit up showing me the violet flame she had in her eyes and then the color changed to blue like how mine were now… I dropped to my knees when I got right in front of her. My hand felt so heavy as I lifted it up and caressed my daughter's cheek. The feeling I had inside of me changed forever and I knew it was the feeling of being complete. I had never felt so damn full in my life, but this was something I would never take advantage of. My father took so much from me, from us but here we were. We showed out not just for ourselves but for my mom, Hina's mom and all those supes who were experimented on.

It was hard being out there and seeing hurt humans that were dying from the virus but as I let everything slow down, I realized one thing… that my own sister, a woman who never had the chance to be free or loved, loved me enough to not only take care of me but to take care of my son. In her taking care of my son, he took care of this little beautiful girl who couldn't be seen by anyone other than her twin. If Phoenix hadn't shared that with me as she matched my flame, I would've never known. I just met her, and I loved her wholeheartedly, I would never turn my back on her, ever again.

I'm so sorry

I said to her telepathically and when I felt the familiar hum, I didn't think as I hugged her tightly.

It's okay. You are everything I've ever imagined too, mama.

I never thought I could ever ugly cry, but this made me do that as I heard her little voice in my head calling me a title, I felt like I never deserved. I would do everything in my power to make sure I never fail her or her brother because they made sure to stay alive long enough for me to meet them. They are more than I could ever ask for.

Chapter 17
Xánur

Thwap I knew that I smacked the shit out of Vali, and I didn't care. I needed him to finally come to. It had been weeks of him healing and I knew how painful it was for him to heal putting his entire body back together. The shock of the slap had him opening his eyes and had I not felt bad for him, I would've laughed. His eyes roamed around as he tried to figure out where he was.

"You're in the palace, my palace." He was very confused. "Not the one you stayed in but my original palace that no one could have but me."

Vali blinked. It was weird looking at him, his hair was longer this time, the auburn color turning much more copper than before, wavy as ever. His eyes shined bright green and the freckles were all over his face. He was different and I didn't know why.

"You're different," I said to him as he sat up from the bed that he was in.

"Different?" He questioned. "I don't feel different, I feel insane… trapped. I can still feel the cage around my mind as we speak. How did you?" Then, as if he went out of focus, the question I wanted to avoid answering was the only one that had me speechless for a moment, "Where is Sirina? Was that her that I saw?"

He ran his fingers through his wavy hair that grew really fast. It was now down his chest when it barely reached the nape of his neck before. I observed him for a moment, then I sighed as I made my way across the bedroom towards a black Victorian looking chair. Who the hell decorated this room? Everything in here had a dark Victorian theme and it was as though I saw it for the first time. I shook my head knowing that I was avoiding Vali's question. The growling in his voice made me turn to face him, he was shifting and now, it clicked. All those times I had seen Vali, not once had he shifted, nor had I felt how powerful he was. It had been so long since he'd even fought a war that I forget about everything, I was so focused on Cin that none of it mattered.

"I am your uncle, answer my question!" He commanded and if I hadn't known him, I would've taken his tone as a threat.

"Uhh… " I put my index finger up, "well, you're Asar's uncle but sure, we're family. I didn't say I wasn't going to answer your question. I'm starting to think that zombie Vali was better than this."

He growled again, this time his fangs appearing and his eyes going completely white as I heard the rumblings of thunder and then lighting strike right after.

"Don't test me, where is she?" He was still sitting on the bed, which was the indication that he wasn't going to attack me just yet.

I avoided his eyes as I focused on a horrible painting of the night sky.

"What's the last thing you remember?" I asked him.

"I crossed over to the other side… I had to save Sirina. I knew she was in trouble and the only way was to give myself up for her but that man, he did something to her. She was in love."

The pain he felt radiated throughout the room. This was possible because Vali wasn't a Nephilim, he was a damn god. Son of Odin and a giantess. I didn't say anything letting him know that whenever he was ready to continue, then he would. After a moment or two, he continued,

"How is it, that my mate? My own mate was able to love someone more than she loved me. At first, I thought it wasn't real but then I felt it through our tether, she loved him Xánur. She loved that bastard wholeheartedly, much more than she did me, but I was a love-sick god, I would've moved Valhalla to her if she ever wanted to see it. Me?" he chuckled like a madman. "I gave myself up for her. Even now, I want to know of her safety."

I sighed not wanting to break his heart even more, but I had to, if he wanted to know the truth. I was only away from Cin for three years, and I was ready to kill any and everything,

"She passed Vali. It's been over twenty-seven years now, she had a daughter with Victor, Hina. The one you saw," then everything became so clear. I faced him, "And now I know why you looked at her like you loved her."

"She...She," he took a breath and out shutting his eyes in the process. The moment his eyes landed on mine, I knew what was going to happen.

Father... tell Uncle Magni, his brother is going to need him. He just learned of what has happened to his mate.

As I finished telepathically telling my father, Vali unleashed a warrior's cry. One that lit up the skies causing a thunderstorm and I just sat there, knowing how painful this was.

****

Lucinda

To say that I felt what Hina and my children felt was an understatement. It was hard to even know how they survived everything, and it hurt me as each sentence was revealed by each of them. I stared at Hina, she was beautiful, but I knew she was just as scarred mentally and physically. Sometimes as she told me everything, she'd pause and Exra would place his little hand over hers then she'd take a deep breathe just like now. I watched as Exra observed her making sure she was mimicking his breathing pattern and unlike earlier when he sat back letting her talk, this time he took over.

"She needs time... this is hard for her," I tilted my head. How did he know that?

"How?" Before I could finish my sentence, Exra answered.

"Nixy and I are tethered to her. We're her protectors."

Hina seemed to be surprised at this as she looked at Exra with a wide-eyed expression.

"You and your sister are my guardians? She's been there the whole time? With you?"

Exra nodded as he stood and wrapped his arms around Hina's neck soothing her while she laid her head on his little shoulder. This seemed like something that happened all the time, and it was too precious. It was beautiful to see that my son protected my sister and his.

Exra began speaking, "Nixy didn't die like everyone thought. Instead, our powers activated even before you gave birth to us. Nixy protected me when she switched positions with me in the womb, and that was why you were in so much pain. She took my place as the first born. The moment our powers activated, it seemed as though she died but she didn't. Her powers activated that night and she became invisible, that's why there was no body to find. She survived because of me, whatever I was fed, she got.　My powers activated a year after, and that's when I first saw her. She explained to me through the link. I don't know how but we talked, and she told me. The first time we merged, I met our father when he popped up in the room. He didn't know what happened, but Nixy saw him standing there. I don't know what made her human again, but it had something to do with you and our father."

At this revelation, Exra let go of Hina as he turned to face Phoenix who sat on the floor still staring up at me. Every so often, she'd tilt her head as if she was taking it all in or as if I would disappear, but little did she know, I watched her from the corner of my eyes making sure that I wouldn't lose her either. I didn't want to ever lose any of them including my sister. I smiled at her as I took a deep breath in and as I got to the floor to sit in front of her, I exhaled.

"I thought I'd never get to see you," Phoenix started, and she caught me by surprise. "I'd dream of you sometimes. I can do that ya know? Just think of you and you'll show up in my dreams. You're just as beautiful as the first time you appeared in there."

The way Phoenix talked about me made me fall in love with her even much more than I could ever say.

"I am?" I said to her as I reached up smoothing out my hair in the messy bun that it was in. I let out a nervous chuckle, "What were we doing in those dreams?"

Phoenix smiled, and I was grateful that such a beautiful little girl was mine. She was the spitting image of Xáne when she smiled. I said it without even realizing it.

"You look so much like your father when you smile," at this, she smiled widely, and she had dimples. "You're so beautiful, I can't believe you're mine."

Phoenix jumped up so quickly I didn't have time to recover as she hugged me, and we fell over to the floor. I laughed hard at her tight hug, even this reminded me of my husband. As if I conjured him, he appeared in front of us. He looked so much bigger as my eyes were fixed on him then a smirk appeared on his face. He winked at me,

"What about me?" He said playfully. "You didn't dream of me, Nixy girl?" The nickname for our daughter made me smile wider.

Phoenix let me go just as fast as she attacked me and leaped up on her feet. I watched as she smiled at her father. She nodded her head at a speed I hadn't seen a supe do before and Xáne laughed.

"It's going to be fun training you two but for now, let's take it one step at a time." Xáne said as he knelt down to be almost eye to eye with his daughter.

This! This was all that I wanted. A family. I had never had one before Xáne and meeting him was the best thing that had ever happened to me.

I caressed his mind with mine, making sure to speak to him in the softest way possible so that our tether could make him feel the love that I felt for him.

Thank you.

He smiled even though he didn't take his eyes off our kids, he replied.

For what... love?

I sighed as I sat up.

For everything. For loving me, this family and the way that even though you tried, you never let me go. I don't know what I would do without you. You complete me.

This time, Xáne's eyes shifted to mine and the love in those pale blue eyes was all I ever and all I'll ever need.

You will always be mine baby. My family, my heart, my soul and even when all else ends, this love of ours will live on for centuries.

With that declaration, my heart exploded. I stood from my place and got closer to him. I grabbed Xáne's face into my hands and kissed him. I kissed him like the world was ending. I made him feel the love that I had for him and I wanted our kids to know that our love was what brought them here and now it was transferred over to them; we will love them even more than we did the first time because these two were the reason we found our way back together. We owed it all to our kids because without them, nothing would ever make sense again.

We were death and fire to everyone else but to our kids and the rest of our family, we were two beings hopelessly in love. Just plain old Xánur and Lucinda Helson, a man and a woman whose souls were made for one another in a world that one side was safe while the other was filled with a virus that not only killed humans but now was killing supes.

Throughout all that, he was Xáne and I was Cin, the only fire that could burn death.

Epilogue
Xánur

I smiled widely as I stood there watching as Exra trained with Phoenix. They were fighting each other, and I knew that was the only way they would learn each other's weaknesses. If they learned that then they could protect each other from that. I observed as Exra who thought he was better at combat than his sister strikes a blow to her chest causing her to fly back a few feet, Cin gasped somewhere from behind me and I shook my head.

"No Lucinda, don't interfere." I stated.

Before she could say anything, Phoenix stood to her feet and charged Exra. She ran at full force. As she ran, her speed increased and then she did the one thing I expected her to do. She made herself invisible, as Exra slowly searched around for her, I saw the little spark of purple as she reappeared in his face with her fist raised, and her elbow cocked back striking him hard in the jaw. I heard the impact it had on him and I cringed, that was going to leave a scar but Exra didn't drop instead, he called on his flames transforming into death's grandson. He wasn't as big as me, but his skin was covered head to toe like mine with the talons appearing.

I couldn't be prouder than I was in this instance as Phoenix joined Exra transforming herself into a dragon shaped flame. It was fascinating to watch as each of them displayed their abilities, and I communicated with them via telepathy.

Now, merge.

Without much thought, they joined hands. This was what the prophecy was truly about. My father's words floated in my mind. These twins were the real reason why Victor didn't want you two to stay together because what they transformed you two into, could make the supernatural world tremble in fear. Victor thought your children were the real threat, but it was the love that you and Cin share... What's love without tragedy?

And tragedy brought heartache, pain and so much dread, but it didn't stop there. No… it made you see who your enemy was and who would stick by you in the times of need. For example, Jaya… she was my enemy from the beginning, but I never saw it. She was always there even before Cin disappeared and it never occurred to me why she was so close to me or how Victor always had the chance to come in and out as he pleased. Jaya was an accomplice, one who died seeking power that never belonged to her. She may have thought that being burnt to a crisp was the end for her but no baby, that was never the end… my father ate up her soul as though it was just a mere appetizer and when he was ready for her to be his dinner, he will spit her back out and make sure to primp, prime and fatten her up with torture to be his ultimate meal.

See that's what happens when you betray or attack a Helson… My eyes scanned the area as I saw Asar further back near the open woods as his eyes fixated on Hina, who sat away from all of us watching the kids in awe.

I should rephrase that statement… Betraying a Helson was one thing but causing a Ragna like Asar to be provoked was a death sentence waiting to happen. I spoke to him through a private frequency where no one else would eavesdrop not even my mate.

Say the word brother, and we will go.

For the first time in weeks, he looked my way. His eyes were full of anger, vengeance and if the spillage of blood has a sight then it would be whatever I saw in Asar's eyes.

I want to end that side of the world once and for all, and if I find one supe that had anything to do with causing my mate to be as distraught as she is… they will die a death so painful, their ancestors will feel it.

He smirked and I matched his expression.

Done.

I could tell Asar remembered something as he looked my way with a weird expression.

There's a part of the prophecy we both ignored.

I was confused, not understanding what he meant.

What part is that?

Asar shook his head.

The part where it says...their offspring are the key to end it all.

I stared at Asar not sure what to say...There were so many questions that I needed the answer to like why Victor did what he did or how? Or the random supes that weren't immune. I faced Hina, she knew all the answers to these questions and the only way we were going to know the answers were if she wanted to tell us.

I turned back to face Asar just in time for him to turn away as Cin touched my elbow, I faced her. She was looking between me and Asar. I quickly distracted her kissing her forehead.

"You know that I'd do anything for you right?"

She sighed,

"Yes, I know." She answered.

"And you know that I'd do anything to make sure you felt safe right?"

Cin nodded her head, "I do baby, I do."

I pulled her in for a tight hug as my eyes found Asar one more time as he just watched Hina. I let Cin go as I cupped her face in my hands, "Then, know this... Asar is going to do any and everything to make sure his mate feels safe. So, trust us?"

"Always."

"I love you Lucinda Helson." I smiled at her as I leaned in.

"I love you too, Xánur Helson." She replied right before I pulled her in for another kiss not giving a damn that the kids were pretending to vomit at our intimacy.

She was my heart, my soul, my mixture of cinnamon and brimstone... above all else, she was my human flame. All Mine.

Again, I ask...What's love without tragedy?

The End

Looking for a publishing home?

After Hours Publications, is accepting submissions from motivated, talented Experienced and Non- Experienced Authors that are excited about spreading Romance. If you have a knack for creating stories in the genres of Contemporary, Interracial, Paranormal, Historical, New Adult, or creating heart felt, drama filled, passionate stories that spotlights the LGBT community we want to hear from you. If you're interested, submit the first 3-4 chapters with your synopsis to Submissions@afterhourspublications.com.

Check out our website for more information:

www.afterhourspublications.com

Be sure to LIKE our After Hours Publications page on Facebook.

KING ELLIE